Flash Fiction

Sheppey Writers' Group

AUP UK
Terrestrial And Universal
Publications

Published in the United Kingdom
TAUP UK
Sheerness
Kent

enquiries@taup.uk

Foreword

By Peter Apps

The layout in this book may seem eccentric but fear not, there is madness to our method.

Our aim was to encourage new writers who have not contributed to our anthologies before so they have been placed at the front of the book. Since the contributions are flash fiction, we've attempted to place them on single pages or starting on an even number so that the full story is front on you. Otherwise, it is in strict alphabetical order unless ...

Of course, it all breaks down if you're reading an ebook, when the stories don't fit or there is an 'R' in the month but we tried.

By James Apps

The question was "how to write a short story that can be easily read on radio in less than three minutes?" The answer was Flash Fiction, a collection of short and very short stories suitable for reading to the public on afternoon radio.

Our aim was to encourage new writers who have not contributed to our anthologies before and also to give the Sheppey Writer's Group another chance to show off their talents. Stories had to be five hundred words or less. We did not ask writers to stick to a theme, and as a result we have collected a variety of stories, some weird, some odd but all reflecting the ideas of the authors. The need to keep them short creates concise stories of high quality and encourage writers to edit their work to fit inside the three minute time slot.

We managed to read some on Sheppey FM radio on some Wednesdays during the "Good Read" section that usually includes a short interview as well as the readings.

We would like to than the contributors and also welcome work from our one time leading light, Wally Newby, and thanks to Dawn Cockburn and Mick Terry of Sheppey FM for inviting us to their show.

Contributors

Amanda Cooper

Side Ward

Donald lay immobile in the hospital bed, his arm in a plaster cast, his head throbbing. The stitches in his left temple and his battered face testament to the savagery of the attack. The last 24 hours had been a blur to him and he just wanted to be left alone to come to terms with what had happened.

To distract himself he looked around the side ward he was in. There were three other beds. One bed was occupied by an enormously overweight man. How do people get so fat wondered Donald as he gazed at the sleeping man who was hooked up to various monitors and oxygen.

The next bed along was occupied by an incredibly frail and apparently ancient gentleman. He lay on his back, mouth slightly open, asleep, or so Donald assumed. Only the gentle rise and fall of his chest indicated that he was still alive.

The bed next to Donald was empty, its sheets and covers neatly made up. There was a jug of water and a bottle of squash on the nightstand which Donald assumed meant it was occupied. Just as Donald looked away an elderly man, in his early seventies, shuffled into the ward on a walking frame.

As he reached the end of Donald's bed he stopped and said "You look like you've been through hell."

Donald found the man's comment strangely comforting but all he could croak in response was, "I have."

"Well you're in good hands here," the man said. "Especially that Nurse Ling". With that the man winked at Donald. "Name's Gordon Holland or "Dutch" to my friends" and with that he shuffled towards the empty bed. Donald closed his eyes but despite his bone crushing weariness sleep eluded him, disturbed by the noises of a busy hospital and with growing irritation, the obese man snoring and snuffling.

Donald wondered how Dutch managed and looked across at his neighbour, surprised to see Dutch's bed empty, bedsheets and covers still neatly tucked in. Donald's chest suddenly tightened and he felt nauseous. He closed his eyes and found himself dreaming.

1

Dutch appeared pushing a wheelchair which he parked next to Donald's bed. "Righto old chap! You ready for liberation?" Donald must have looked puzzled as Dutch went on, "Hop in, we're leaving". Donald found himself sitting up easily, no pain, which he thought was strange but then it was a dream. He climbed out of bed and into the wheelchair. Like two naughty schoolboys the two elderly men made their way out of the hospital and into the night.

Ward rounds an hour later sent the night staff calling for the on call Doctor. "It's Mr Cope. We found him deceased on our routine check. No indication previously that he was in any particular difficulties. Must have been his heart Doctor. Should we let patient admin know we now have two beds free on Poplar Ward?"

Malcolm R Gibbs

Share

That looks and smells lovely. Please can I have some?

Yes, I know I didn't eat my tea but I would really like some of that. I promise to eat every little piece and I'll definitely eat my own tea afterwards, honestly.

What do you mean 'there's nothing left'? Look at what you've got piled on your plate; you can't possibly need to eat all of that. How about sharing some with me? (HUFF)

I really do love you, you know. Please can I have some, just a little bit will do. I'm so hungry, I haven't eaten for ages. Please, please.

How can you be so wicked as to sit there and keep putting that lovely food in your mouth without offering me some?

Share, listen to me, share. (HUFF) You're ignoring me aren't you?

Yes, yes, you keep telling me that I have my own tea but I don't want it, I want what you've got.

I promise to be good for ever and ever if you just let me have a little bit, just a taste, just a morsel. (HUFF) I just don't know how you can be so selfish.

How can you be so cruel? (HUFF)

No, no don't eat too quickly, you'll eat it all up then there will be nothing left. (HUFF) It will serve you right if you get indigestion.

Ah, see I said you couldn't eat it all, your eyes were bigger than your belly. You're going to leave some, I know you are.

Told you, told you, now stop teasing and give me that.

Wait where are you going, where are you taking that? I'm coming too.

"Mum, how can I eat my tea when the bloody dog keeps staring at me all the time?"

Malcolm R Gibbs

Bad 'n's

The young scientist had discovered the micro-organisms by accident but they were evil and in the wrong hands could be catastrophic so he had hidden them from the world. Yet over the years, eleven people had died in excruciating pain. Their agony lasting until their hearts gave out. Death Certificates said 'Cause of Death: Heart Failure'.

People said "Good riddance".

~~~

Osteoarthritis had slowly crippled John Kirbishly eventually forcing him to give up work but there were some tasks that he was still determined to do, no matter what the pain. Each week, relying heavily on two walking sticks, he slowly walked to Mr and Mrs Khan's corner shop. John liked the Khans; they couldn't do enough to help him.

Like many terraced houses John's back garden resembled a small courtyard. But this courtyard was a glorious array of colours and wonderful smells, a memorial to his wife who had been taken far too early.

In one corner stood the small ceramic elf that Catherine had teasingly given to him many years ago. He hated the damn thing but still smiled every time he looked at it.

On the day that the house next door changed hands he saw the rusty old van pull up. Out climbed a scruffy man and an equally scruffy woman. As they approached, the woman looked across and saw John.

"Who do you think you're staring at you old git?" she shouted and gestured with her middle finger.

"Oh dear," he thought. "I hope that's not a bad omen."

People spoke more and more about the aggravation and upset they were causing but John himself had not seen anything; although he certainly heard the shouting and arguments in the most disgusting language.

When Mr Kahn caught the woman stealing from his shop, he had confronted her. The husband responded by viciously beating Mr Kahn but, despite his injuries, no charges were brought against his attacker.

John Kirbishly knew...

Drawing back his curtains, he immediately saw the damage. His

4

beautiful garden had been wrecked. Two days of pain brought the garden back into shape but Catherine's little elf was beyond repair.

With lights out John watched two shadowy figures climb over the wall. Within minutes all his work was undone.

John Kirbishly knew…

The pain was almost unbearable as he again repaired the damage.

"Don't worry Catherine, everything will be alright."

When dusk fell, he took a small canister from his fridge. In the darkness, John moved slowly down the garden and carefully placed a minute dab of liquid on the wall; the virus would spread rapidly for about an hour then die if not absorbed by a host. John expected the visitors to climb over within that time. He was not disappointed.

Their screams kept him awake all night but he didn't mind because John Kirbishly knew… they were bad 'ns.

He smiled "An old git maybe, but an old git who's a mass murderer…"

Malcolm R Gibbs

The Man

Life had given Timothy Budden a bad deal. Born blind and paralysed from the waist down; caring for him had been very difficult for his parents. Timothy, despite all of his problems, was such a happy and bubbly little boy. Like many children, Timothy had his make believe friend who he spoke to regularly. His parents were often concerned that the friend never had a name, Timothy always referred to his friend as 'the man'. It also puzzled them that Timothy always spoke to his friend in a strange language; nothing like they had heard before.

At the age of five, life dealt another blow. Professor Drake had been Timothy's specialist since the boy's birth. As he sat in his office with Mr and Mrs Budden it reminded him of five years earlier.

"Sadly, I to have to tell you that a scan shows Timothy has a brain tumour." He paused momentarily. "And I'm sorry to add that we are unable to operate on the tumour because it would be far too dangerous for him."

"What about somewhere else?" Mr Budden asked with an obvious desperation."

"Believe me when I say that it is impossible for anyone to operate in Timothy's case."

As his condition worsened, Timothy Budden was admitted to hospital.

On the day things changed, Mr and Mrs Budden arrived at Timothy's small side ward early; only to find their son's bed empty. Mr Budden ran to the nursing desk.

"What's happened to Timmy? You should have called us, not just removed his body."

"Mr Budden, please calm down." the young nurse tried to quieten him. "Nothing's happened; Timothy is fast asleep in his bed."

"No he isn't."

They both hurried along to the room where Mrs Budden laid crying on the empty bed. The nurse hit the emergency button and all three left Timmy's room on a panic driven search.

"Timothy Budden is missing." The nurse reported.

When they returned to his room, they found Timothy Budden lying on his bed.

"Timmy, what happened? Where did you go?" Mrs Budden cuddled him tight.

"I went with the man."

"Timmy, we don't understand." His mother held his shoulders "The man took me to the hospital."

"Hospital, what do you mean hospital?"

"The hospital that is a long, long way from here."

Professor Drake marched into the room with his usual air of authority.

"What's going on here young man?" he asked.

Timothy looked towards him. "The man made me all better."

"Did he now? I think we will have to check that out." Turning to the nurse, "Wheelchair please, nurse."

"I don't need it." And Timothy Budden jumped off of the bed.

As well as walking and being able to see, a scan later showed that the tumour had completely disappeared.

What happened on that day will always be a mystery to everyone; except, of course, Timothy Budden... and 'the man'.

Selina Jobbins

Shadow of a Stalker

Summer was approaching and with local colleges winding down, myself and Johnny were now the only two people at the bus stop. Johnny was a boy of few words though we did talk about his religious duties and upcoming summer sabbatical as a Jehovah Witness. Although engrossed in conversation I noticed an unusual looking figure fading in and out of the background to my right. He seemed to be a male in his early fifties, tall and gaunt, strikingly nervous and unable to stand still.

Johnny always looked out for the bus and stood aside to allow me on first. I saw the bus approaching, while the creepy figure sidled towards me. He was wearing a thick coat jacket though the weather was warm and I could make out old-fashioned thick lensed glasses.

As the bus stopped with a hiss of brakes and conversation abruptly ground to a halt, the man approached me, touching my shoulder and asking for the time. I shuddered. Not one to wear a watch I knew the bus was never late and hastily replied, 'Eight-thirty'.

I wasted no time getting on the bus and showing my pass, before being greeted by one of my extremely chatty friends who I had known since Primary School. Whilst she excitedly recalled what she would be doing in the last few days of college, I studied the man I now feared. He searched his pocket for the exact change then spotted me and walked towards me. He sat in the only empty seat, just behind me next to Johnny. Johnny had his head phones on and was blissfully unaware of his strange seating partner.

With only ten per cent of my brain tuning into the conversation I found myself in flight mode, wondering how I might escape this man whose breath I could feel against my neck. I knew that two buses met alongside the stops where I planned to get off and a surge of college students would stampede out of each bus. With the bus starting to slow, I stood to get ahead of the crowd, and my friend closely followed me.

8

As we were swept into the high street, I looked behind me to see the man looking around for me. Instinctively, as the passengers scattered, I merged with the public in the High Street. Joining up with a couple of male friends I felt safe enough to look back two or three times until I was sure he was gone. *Something* told me I wouldn't see him again.

Wally Newby

Once Upon A Time

It was quiet at breakfast. The wife was deep in thought about her shopping necessities while the husband sat contemplating a letter that had come in the morning past. He looked across at his wife.

"Pass the marmalade."

"Here ... Who's the letter from ?"

"The Water Board."

"The Water Board! What do they want?"

"They're saying that we are going to be cut off today and tomorrow. Seems they have to do urgent repairs to the mains along the road."

"We're going to be cut off ! How are we going to get fresh water then? They can't just cut us off like that!"

"No... They're saying here that standpipes will be accessible at several places in the area. There's a list here ... Norton's Farm seems to be the nearest."

"But that's a quarter of a mile up the hill."

"No... It'll be OK. It'll be shorter by taking the footpath."

"What a bloomin' nerve shutting us off. And without any warning. nor nothing."

"Yeah, I agree ... Can't see we can do much about it though. We can have a moan, l suppose. Lodge an official complaint, but if it's an emergency, don't think we'd have a leg to stand on."

"Bloody' inconvenient though. We'll have to take a couple of buckets up to Nortons."

"Yeah... Might be best to take one, and make two journeys."

"Yes ... You could be right. Come on then, let's go before the rain starts again."

"Careful ... Careful."

"I am being careful."

"Well, be more careful You're spilling all the water."

"I can 't help it. This bucket's heavy, and it's bloomin' steep here."

" Here, let me help."

"Alright ... No, don't lift it. Just steady the bucket. Stop it swinging."

"It's hard just keeping me balance."

"OK Careful."

"I'm wearing the wrong shoes for this. I keep sliding."

"Should have worn your trainers."

"Yeah ... OH ... OH ... Look out ... Ahhhhh, bugger."

" MIND OUT ... OOOOOH ! ... Hold it ..."

"YOU STUPID ... AAAHHHHI—Ilfll!"

"I SAID ... OOOOOhhhhm NOOOOO!"

"Help, Help, please help me up."

"I can't ... Can you help me up ? Oh God, you're bleeding."

"My head hurts. Is it bad?"

"Horrible. I'll call an Ambulance."

"Oh No ... No ... Just let me get home to bed."

" You stay there."

" No ... l'm alright ... I know what's best."

" JACK....YOU .....YOU'RE STUPID!!! Aunt Maisey's Holistic treatment is useless."

" It's not."

" Vinegar and Brown Paper ... urrgh!"

Wally Newby

Cottage For Sale

The window pane rattled. Things needed to be done. He'd expected that. Saunders, the estate agent, droned on. 'Yes, 18th Century, with later additions, of course. First built as a bakery. The ovens were removed when the kitchen was built, but the ironwork of the shelves is still on the pantry wall."

Upstairs, the bedrooms were small but adequate, and a bathroom had been added. A bit tatty, Clive thought, but that could be modernised. However, he was puzzled by a large cupboard on the landing. An airing cupboard, maybe? He turned to Saunders.

"There's a boiler in the kitchen and I've seen radiators, but where's the hot water tank?"

"Oh, it's in the loft," the agent chortled, 'I'll switch on the boiler, you can see it all working." And so saying, disappeared downstairs.

Clive peered into the cupboard. It wasn't deep, but the back boarding appeared to be loose. He pushed it, and it moved. He pushed harder and suddenly the hinged back fell away. Clive stumbled, lost his balance and fell, yelling, head-first, into a gaping black hole. The door slammed and he screamed as he landed upon something squelchy. it was pitch black, and the stench was terrible. He touched something. A cold, sticky face amid damp tattered clothing. He screamed.

"Aaaaaahh!"

Surely Saunders would be back by now? He yelled again.

"HELP!"

But there was no response.

Sunders stood on the landing, puzzled.

"Oh No,' he groaned, 'He's gone, disappeared, just like the other clients."

Memory Lane

In the days before County Cricket succumbed to Mammon, 1st XIs would often spend their Sundays playing against village teams. In 1961, I lived in a Kent village whose team was quite good, but even so, I was astonished to find that on a certain date, we would be facing the County 1st XI at our local recreation ground.

On the day, we were six deep on the grass lining the boundary rope, and applauded heartily' as Colin Cowdrey, Alan Knott, Brian Luckhurst and other well-known County players came trotting out of our small pavilion. And was that a young Mike Denness among them? We couldn't believe our eyes, and on our own 'dung heap' at that.

We batted first, and the applause was tremendous when someone scored a boundary which, sadly, was not that often! Knotty, ever the comedian, gave a display behind the stumps that enabled a few of our batsmen to stay at the crease, when they ought to have been 'out'. Sadly I cannot recall any bowler's names, nevertheless, we put up a tidy score with a creditable performance. However, what we were waiting for came after the tea break. Cowdrey and Luckhurst facing our 'demon bowlers', and what a game it was !

We were treated to a wonderful performance, with stroke play beyond belief. Some of our bowlers were successful but eventually' Cowdrey, and others surrendered their wickets and the result of the match was decided by a tussle with the tail-enders.

The score was irrelevant. What mattered was the spirit of the match, and Oh, didn't we enjoy it! Our lads had tested their metal against some of the top names in the country, and we had seen our heroes in the flesh, playing cricket at its very best.

Wally Newby

Souvenirs

Sally made her way out into the garden. She must catch the Gardener before he left.

"Hey," she called, "Could you wait a moment. Don't go."

The Gardener looked up, and waited, as she shuffled down the path.

"Oh thank you," she gasped, "Sorry to trouble you, but ... have you seen a small pile of stones? They were on the bird bath the other day, and now I can't find them."

"Oh. What, about a dozen flints and pebbles: I thought they were just stones. I dumped them in a rubbish sack. Did you want to keep them?"

"Oh yes, very much so, they are my favourites."

The young man smiled. "I didn't think anyone could have favourite stones."

"Ah well, you see, they are special. I brought them here, and they mean a lot to me."

"Oh, I'm so sorry. I'll find them for you, but why are they so special ?"

"Ah ... It's a long story ... Vince Taylor came with the Canadians, during the war. They were billeted on us. Off course, we didn't know about D Day then, but we knew something was up, with troops everywhere. We had horses on the farm then, and disaster struck when Rosie, the big mare, went lame. Dad was trying to see what was wrong with her, when some of the troops arrived. Vince came over and asked what was wrong. Dad explained, and was surprised when Vince asked if he could examine the horse. Apparently, in civilian life, he was a farrier. He spoke quietly to Rosie, stroked her, and before long had her rolling on the ground while he worked on the hoof, draining a septic swelling. Two days later, Rosie was on her feet, right as rain ... I helped Vince when he came to check on Rosie over the next weeks, and I knew he had taken a shine to me. We fell in love ... Simple as that.

"A few weeks later, he came to the farm and asked me to go

14

for a walk. He was quiet. Something was happening. They'd got their orders. They'd be gone in a few days.

"We sat on the bench in the Churchyard, silent. We held each other close, then Vince reached down and picked up a few stones from the pathway.

"Hold these for me, please ... just until I come back."

He never did. He's buried in Normandy!'

Mike Pearce

Mr Jacobs' Garden

I watched Mr Jacobs from the window as he pottered in the garden.

Since the passing of his soul mate Rose, the garden is where he is happiest. It is where he spends most of his time, especially since he is now always joined by a Robin, who Mr Jacobs tells me is the spirit of his beloved Rose.

Every day, I blink away the tears welling in my eyes as I watch him chatting away to his feathered gardening assistant, knowing the comfort this brings to him and helping to ease the heartache of his loss.

As usual, I headed outside to top up various wildlife feeders and ask Mr Jacobs if there is anything I can get for him when I visit the shops. The reply was the same as it was on most occasions, "no thank you my dear". My question always had double intention, firstly, to see if I could help with the grocery needs and secondly, to make conversation.

I commented on the beauty of his flower beds. He credited his assistant Rose for helping him to maintain such a colourful display. The Robin, perched on the fence between us, seemed to be listening intently, twisting and turning its head as we conversed.

The following morning, I once again looked out into Mr Jacobs' garden, pausing to admire the array of floral colour, with each flower looking proud to be part of such a magnificent display.

Mr Jacobs was not yet in attendance, which was not unusual, his time in the garden was frequent but not on a strict schedule.

I continued with my day but grew more uneasy with every glance out of the window that showed no sign of Mr Jacobs.

As late afternoon approached, I felt the need to see if all was well. I knocked at Mr Jacobs's door and waited. After several attempts drew no response, I returned to my house. Flicking through my contacts book, I called to his daughter, who informed me that they spoke only last night and that she would be coming to check on him immediately.

I watched as she arrived with her husband. With the expected anxious expressions etched on their faces, they used their key to enter Mr Jacobs home. With butterflies in my stomach, I waited, looking out occasionally to see if all was well.

I tried to busy myself, wondering what was happening, when I was startled by the doorbell. It was Mr Jacobs' son-in-law. The news was devastating. Mr Jacobs had passed in his sleep.

I thought about nothing else for the rest of the day, shedding many a tear along the way.

The morning after, I looked out into Mr Jacobs' garden as usual. I gave a sharp intake of breath at what I saw and headed out into my garden.

The two Robins sat perched on the fence as I approached. "Good morning Mr and Mrs Jacobs." I said. "The garden looks beautiful."

Val Smith

Bugged

One Monday morning my husband, Richard, drove me to the garden centre. At first, it was quite a grey day, but as the day went on it got sunnier and warmer. We had a stroll around the gardens, Richard was a keen gardener and we had just moved into a bungalow which was to be our retirement home. The new garden was quite, large so Richard had some grand plans for it. We walked round the ponds where yellow lilies floated on the water. Then I looked at the signs 'Danger - Deep Water' and I said to myself 'very deep, always has been'. As we rested on a bench, a trio of elderly ladies were looking at the flowerbed behind.

"Oh I do like those plants there, but I can never remember their name." Then another voice said,

"I love the way they do the planting here." Then the third woman suddenly said: "There could be a body around here, that's why the plants are growing so well." They all laughed and carried on around the gardens.

I gave a small shiver even though the sun was warm. Then my mind went back to the first time I had visited this place. That November night when I had driven my cheating husband here, drugged, so he was helpless. How I had got him out of the car, stumbling like a drunk. There were the signs 'Danger - Deep Water'. I managed to get him close to the edge then I gave him a shove and in he went. He floundered for a few minutes then he was gone. I drove home and got rid of all his things. I told our families he had left me for another woman. In fact, I said he had been having a string of affairs throughout most of our marriage.

His parents were very upset, they kept waiting for a phone call or letter. I think they hired a private detective, but of course he came back saying that he could not find any trace of David.

I got on with my life as a nurse and later l met Richard who was my solicitor and had helped me through my divorce. He was a kind, gentle man and in good time we were married. We have two lovely, children; a boy and a girl, and now, we have grandchildren too. Life has been good to me.

I looked at dear Richard and said "Come on Love let's go and choose the plants for our new garden." He smiled as arm in arm we walked to the nursery. The woman had been right about a body being buried in the gardens. It was a long time ago, and David must be a skeleton by now.

Tony Stubley

Words – Worth, A Lesson in Loquaciousness

Well!, what do you know?, the 'homework' set for the creative writing group that I attend, is to utilise nine words from a list generated by the group, incorporating them into a 500 word story, brilliant. I love using vocabulary, enjoying the sound of words, the effect that they can have on an audience.

So what delights did we come up with?

MELLIFLUOUS: A poetic, flowing, sweet tasting word that sounds like it should drip from your mouth in a honey dewed accent. A good word to sweeten the tone of the exercise ... so what's next?

FIDGET: A bumptious, irritant of a word, loaded with negativity. I mean you never ask someone TO fidget do you?

ATTIC: Comes next, a dark, dusty word. Old and musty, a word at the top of the lexicon to make you cough and splutter as you ruminate on forbidden childhood expeditions into unknown territory.

INEFFABLE: Follows, a word of the unspeakable, the unnamed, unloved by the publishing world save Choasium and the Black Library. A word favoured by Lovecraft and his disciples.

BLURRING: A word to focus our efforts no less, clarity chides caution. A word to confuse the mix, to coalesce our thoughts.

PERNICIOUS: A favoured word of mine, not to be confused with another of my favourite words, PERFIDIOUS as in Perfidious Albion, although I have never been perfidious myself, Albion being my craft name. Pernicious, a word I first encountered in the early 90's due to the Vampyre Societies magazine, 'Pernicious Anaemia'. I chose this word!

THUNDERSTORM: I love thunderstorms, nothing better than sitting in a darkened room listening to Thor and watching Mjolnir strike the heavens. Riders on the Storm by the Doors and Rain by The Cult invoke these sensations in me as I listen to them in a darkened room lit only by candlelight with the aroma of incense permeating the ambiance.

MOTEL: Bates Motel, Psycho, Crossroads, Benny, Meg Mortimer, Amy Turtle, Adam Chance and Scottish chef Hughie McFee (the last two whom I've met!). Shame it wasn't Hotel though as I could have used it as an excuse to shoe horn a reference to 'Hotel California' into my smorgasbord of linguistic delights.

DAMP: The last word!. Moist, sodden, a word drenched in sexual connotations, drowning in a sea of innuendo. As featured in the title of that wonderful TV Series, that vehicle for the timeless talents of Leonard Rossiter- Rising Damp.

And that, my friends, completes the list. It only remains for me now to work out how to make sense of these words in such a way as to introduce them into some sort of narrative that will enhance a worthwhile story!

Tony Stubley

A Game Called Echo.

A dead moon falling, rain fills the asylum...

Listen to my voice, I can't remember, I just can't recall it with any certain clarity. Why do I dream of wires? Maybe it was the car crash, maybe it was the war - vague memories of being a patched up veteran, playing cards in a run down back room in Paris with a friend called 'Five'. Was I really there or did I just hear about it? Is it a rogue memory, was it part of THE Plan or just a jagged fragment of a half remembered instalment of the information films that we were shown at the Air Crash Bureau?

Whatever it was, it still clings to me like a shadow in vain. Remind me to smile as my mind rips with the excruciating pain that I endure every day, I die - You die but still it lingers in the subconscious. What about you? Do you remember back then? - I'm not so sure that I really do, memories like replicas of lives past. Do you remember that I was vapour, not a pure, solid, breathing macho man. Five?, was he real or are friends electric, not real flesh and blood entities like me and you? Well, I assume that you and I are made of flesh and blood. Have I now passed into that stage of existence? The one perfect lie.

We are glass, we are so fragile that we all pass into nothingness at the end. Jo- the waiter hovered nearby "Do you need the service?" he enquired in his flat, expressionless, robotic voice.

This wreckage of my personality continues to dredge up past indiscretions of the fallen M.E. down in the park. Echo park, when I was part of the Tube Army, lost amongst the cars and the never ending music for chameleons. Those storm troopers in drag parading in their stiletto heels and jackboots marching to the rhythm of the evening. So, so long ago, and now there's just me in this complex metal labyrinth, trying to escape from my prison moon as I sleep by windows, nameless and forgotten.

The iceman comes. Please push no more. You are in my vision as now, me, I disconnect from you. I finally know what it is that I must do, what my mission is as I set the controls for the heart of the sun and bid you good night. Finally, I am to become a dead son rising!

Sanity Clause

The stairs to the shuttered room creaked as the three of us approached the landing, full of squalor, pictures hung on the wall of deceased family members.

The trip to my late uncle's château had been uneventful until the discovery of the room. As one, we decided to hunt out it's contents, fast - as the skies began to darken outside, the carcass of the sun obscured by black portent filled clouds.

Rain fell, lightening crashed, the stillness echoed and resonated in my brain as I began to envisage the gore of sliced meat awaiting us. I had felt the room before I found it, it's presence had gorged itself upon my mind, feeding me images of wanton feasting: the death of my sanity was close at hand. The door suddenly burst open.

"Sorry to barge in like this," uttered my brother "But you're wanted urgently on the telephone".

I apologised profusely to my fellow investigators and put down my dice and left the room, temporarily putting a halt to our game of 'Call of Cthulhu as I went downstairs to take my phone call.

Three Ultra Short Stories
Ice Scream

Hot sun blazing down, making her feel uncomfortable, the little girl visibly brightens up as she hears the familiar chimes of her favourite ice cream van approaching.

Her mouth waters in eager anticipation of the treat waiting in store. Slowly the van eases around the corner and comes to a standstill as it comes to a standstill opposite.

Excitement mounts within her as she runs out into the road - shame she never saw the car that hit her as she stepped out in front of it - dying for that ice cream!.

~~~

Not A Lotto Luck

10, 12, 13,19,31,46, the balls came out of the lottery machine one by one. I blinked and repeated them out aloud, 10,12,13,19,31,46- yes!, my numbers, all six of them and I began to weep with uncontrolled joy.

Only then did I realise that I had forgotten to renew my ticket for that day's draw!.

~~~

Death of a Leaping Horseman

The noise of the tank's engine and the oil that lubricated it assailed my senses. I sat stiffly, in the darkened interior of the metal machine peering out of the small vision hatch. The glare of the white undulating snow blinded me as the claustrophobia began to hit home.

Scrambling madly, I fought back my terror and made for the turret's hatch, I pushed it open, emerging into the fresh, clean, beautiful air. A shot rang out and I fell backwards into the darkness that engulfed me as my life began to ebb away.

The Story of He and She

"You embarrassed me this evening." he said

"Really! How?" He asked

"By your platitudinous piffle" she replied

"What do you mean by that?" he enquired

"Oh you know, you sung his praises like a congregational choir at evensong." She answered, "and it was really apparent that every word was hollow, false."

"Well, you know that, but I think that he is so dumb that he really didn't understand." he defended himself

"Oh!" she gasped exasperated "But the rest of them did, his advisers are now probably sat down with him, explaining its meaning to him - and you, my love, will be left to suffer the fall-out."

"You're so pessimistic," he admonished. "Don't worry, I've got 'protection' around me. Do you really think that I'd do something like that if I hadn't already thought of the possible consequences and had taken steps to nullify them?"

"I do sometimes wonder." she retorted "I really do. In your quest to tilt at windmills, I do worry that one day you'll get too far ahead of the game and find yourself unseated from your steed."

"Don't worry about that my lady, my steed, as you so eloquently put it, is built for speed. By the time anyone ever catches up with me, the field will be so full of fallen reputations that no-one will want to, let alone be able to unseat me for fear of joining them." He smiled like the political assassin that he was.

"Just be careful that's all I'm asking." she pleaded

"Of course, what do you expect?" He looked at her and lent in close for a kiss " After all, I learnt from a master or should I say mistress didn't I?"

"Yes. Yes, you did." She managed as her lips found his.

Frederick E Woodworth

Le Maison Blanc

Anton de Plume paced the room like a caged animal cursing his stupidity. He'd seen the hotel several times on his travels and it looked discrete enough. Le Maison Blanc was only ten minutes from the station and seemed an ideal set-up. From the front it seemed quite acceptable but his room at the back of the hotel was anything but white. It was a dirty sooty grey that smelt of smoke. It had seemed an ideal opportunity as the whole of France celebrated Liberation Day. Trouble was, the S.N.L.R. seemed to be celebrating it too! He opened the window and looked down on to the double tracked railway some eighty fee below. It was now well after eleven with no sign of a train passing in either direction. This was bad – really bad! They had just three hours to get back. One hundred and eighty kilometres separated them from their home town – it could have been a thousand kilometres for all he cared! He looked at Claudette's voluptuous breasts remembering their night of passion, for she was still not yet fully dressed, and his throat felt dry, but only for a moment. She threw the timetable to the floor in frustration and cursed.

"What the hell are we going to do!" She wailed. People had been shot for less. Here was she, chief of staff's wife having an affair with the head of the police. It had seemed a perfect set-up. Her husband was accompanying De Gaulle in Paris while his wife was in Calais. They'd managed to keep their affair a secret but now it could well blow up in their faces. They had to get out – and fast.

"When is the next train due?" He asked reception in an almost pleading manner.

"Liberation. It is a day of great rejoicing for the whole of France! Things will not get back to normal for weeks." Came the reply.

Just then he heard the commotion going on outside with armed guards standing to attention. He turned white and shot up to his room.

"Get you clothes on and quick! We've got to use the fire escape. They'll be here any minute."

Just as they prepared to leave there was a loud rap at the door.

"Ye ... yes?" He stammered.

"Gendarmes – Papers, please!"

Frederick E Woodworth

The Eyes Have It

Sam Summit woke with a start from his afternoon siesta to find a balaclava clad young man riffling through his living room cabinet. He cursed at his stupidity at having left the patio doors slightly ajar. An opportunist thief out to get what he could. An amateur - that was obvious, but still annoying. At eighty-four, he was no match. He'd have to handle this character carefully.

"Good afternoon!" he called out standing a safe distance away. The young lad screamed as he spun round, his eyes wild with terror.

"Looking for anything in particular are we, or just mooching around? Try ringing the front door next time and I'd let you in."

"Shut it, man! I'm bigger than you!" Peter nodded.

"I'll grant you that. You're not afraid of anybody, which is why you hide behind a balaclava. You look quite ridiculous, like a gone wrong version of Benny from Crossroads."

"I don't like you, man. You're too smooth by far."

"It comes with the job. I'm in reps."

"Reps?"

"Yes, Reps - repertoire to give it, it's correct title. Your woolly hat is doing nothing to hide you because you're revealing the one thing you cannot change - your eyes. They reveal everything about you from day one. Every time you take drugs it shows up on your iris and cannot be undone. I know all about people's eyes. I make it my job. If you open the second drawer, you'll see what I mean. 'The eyes have it' so goes the cliché."

He cautiously did as he was told and found it was full of photographs of people's eyes, with writing on the back, many of them celebrities like Ken Dodd and Lulu.

"Jeez man, what's with this set-up?"

"Good practise for me, this. Take out ten photos and I'll bet you ten pounds I can name every one. You game for a tenner?"

"I don't like this, man. You give me the creeps."

"I told you, I'm a pro. I'm used to talking on stage. Been doing it all my working life. One final thing. Before you go, I don't know or don't care who you are, I'd like to take a snap of your eyes for the record."

The agreed test went ahead. He got every one correct.

"Now what we agreed upon - your eyes."

Fifteen minutes later there was a buzz at the door. Sam casually answered it to five police officers, one of whom was armed with a Tazer.

"You won't need that." he laughed. "He's taking a nap on the sun lounger out on the verandah." They smiled, and then laughed heartily as they had to wake him up and handcuffed him before carting him off. Still groggy on his legs, he wasn't quite sure what was happening. Sam smiled handing the police his business card bearing the legend:

> Anxious? Depressed?
> Super Sammy Summit
> Hypnotist extraordinaire
> Private consultations undertaken.

Beachy Head Incident

David Hart was driving at a sedate speed along Beachy Head Road. Suddenly he was forced to slam on the brakes as a couple of young girls jumped off the grass verge right in front of him and then started hammering on the windscreen, panic etched on their faces.

"Hey! What the hell are you playing at?"

"Please! There's a woman about to throw herself off the cliff. She's right on the edge." He groaned heavily - bloody kids.

"Calm down. What's this all about? She's probably just looking at the lighthouse."

"It's true!" Chorused the second one. "She'd been crying and told us to go away." This was serious."

"Get in!" He barked, as he turned on his blue flashing lights.

"Bravo one-five to control. Heading for Beachy Head lighthouse. investigating a potential suicide. One-five out."

He took off his clip-on tie and unbuttoned his shirt to look as casual as possible. He also started taking photographs of nothing in particular with a digital camera, casually walking in her direction but it was hopeless. She'd spotted him a mile off and immediately became aggressive.

"Back off! You're a copper! Who sent you? Who sent you?" He tried to look round casually feigning innocence as if she might be addressing somebody else but it was no good - she knew.

"Don't come simple with me! Somebody sent you to try to talk me down. Well it won't work."

"Alright, so I'm a copper. A couple of girls were panicking and started hammering on my windscreen. it's my job to investigate these things. Look, can you not stand right on the edge? There are cracks where you're standing and if they give way, ready or not, you're going to take a five-and-a-half second flight to nowhere. I wouldn't be able to grab you even if I wanted to - there's forty feet between. I'm not Superman or Tom Cruise. I'm just a normal copper."

"You're trying to talk me down. I can't take any more."

"Lady, you're in control, not me. l don't know your problem or even your name. Let me get a bit closer to you so that I don't have to shout. By the way, my name's Dave." She shrugged her shoulders uninterested. Just then there were three loud bleeps on his transmitter. He pressed it to his ear, smiled and, turning round, raised his arm.

"You can't take any more, and neither can I. I'll make a deal with you. If you promise not to commit suicide until tomorrow I'll buy you a steak with all the trimmings. Is that a deal?" She laughed heartily.

"You're on! We'll use my car, it's easier. Give me an hour to clean myself up. I look a mess." He laughed and helped her up as they both made their way to where the outside film unit was based along with vans and tents where people were wrapping things up for the day.

Candyfloss & Popcorn

Derek Matthews rubbed his bloodshot eyes and went through everything on his computer with a toothpick.

"How's it going?" Asked Sandra, his sidekick, handing him a mug of black coffee.

"You won't believe just how close we are. Got to be careful though. Question: How old are you? Answer: 'Thirteen.' Reasonable, I suppose. Although make a note, we can't slip up like last time. Four months work down the drain.

"Who's your favourite pop star? Answer: 'Madonna.' Fair enough. Now this is where it gets tricky: What colour are your knickers? What's the answer? What do I put?" Sandra went through the highlighted areas of Q's & A's. and thought hard.

"Pink, just like my face, cheeky bugger L.O.L. Careful though, PAW."

"PAW?"

"PAW - Parents Are Watching. How long did it take to get to this stage?"

"Five weeks, Sandy, you are going on a date. Big Mac and French fries. Half-ten."

"Good God, no. Far too late. She's only meant to be thirteen, remember. Try half-eight."

"OK, half-eight it is. Next Friday."

"Answer: See ya there — don't let on." Derek punched the air with all the force he could muster.

"Yes - yes - yes! We've got him! Third one this month." The triumph was short-lived though. His eyes clouded over as he cupped his face in his hands. Tears rolled freely down his cheeks.

"Oh God. How I hate this job. I really do." He buried his face in Sandra's blouse, knowing everybody else had gone home, and knowing full well nothing he ever said would ever go further.

"I loved her. I really did. She was a niece in a million. l loved her like the daughter I never had. Twelve. I ask you. She was just bloody twelve! Groomed, raped, then dumped in a ditch. God how I'd love to strangle every paedophile and pervert with my bare hands. I'd dig their

32

bloody eyes out! l really would." He slammed both of his fists hard onto his desk, trembling.

"But you won't Derek, because without you, there'd be no stopping them. We need you, Derek. We need you like we've never needed anybody ever before. You're the rock this place is built on. You're pulling in an average of three a month. Don't throw it all away for nothing."

Derek fought hard to regain his composure.

"I'm sorry about that, but you see, Sharon would have been fourteen next week. They say time is a great healer, but the pain goes on forever. He was already an old man when we got him, so he'll die in jail before going straight to Hell, but my Sharon will never age. She will always be twelve. She will be alive in my heart forever."

Derek wiped the tears from his eyes before kissing the framed photo by his desk and shutting down his machine.

"Come on. It's late." She said. "I'll drive you home."

The Forfeit

Following a spate of shoplifting, Foodrite International decided to bring in extra security. There was no shortage of security companies out there supplying such services but they were expensive with no money back guarantees so it was decided to expand on their staff. One applicant was particularly confident, pointing out that he had had previous experience in all major retailers and had also come from a military background.

"I know the score." He replied confidently to most of the questions put before him. He knew the CCTV system inside out and also the best area to watch the customers.

"There's one!" He hissed to the manager, leading him to one side. "See, their eyes are everywhere except on what they're buying. They're trying to suss out where the cameras are." Impressed he watched as he caught her leaving the store red-handed, only to be frog-marched back into the security room.

"Please, it was an accident. A mistake. Here, I'll pay for it now."

"You're dead right, lady. It was a mistake. Tell that to the magistrate. He'll understand."

Profits increased dramatically. It was then that an anonymous letter arrived addressed to John McCullock marked private & confidential. He read the letter several times before looking it away in his safe. Stone faced he left the office.

Later that week another person was caught putting goods into her bag without paying for them and was promptly escorted back into the security room by him and his accomplice.

"Please, there's been a mistake. My husband's a local MP. Oh God," she wailed. "If this gets out, not only will he lose his job, he'll leave me. Please, let me pay for this."

"No way. You say he's an MP? I shouldn't do this but seeing as my colleague's out of the office — and will be for some considerable time looking for a non-existent form I don't see why we shouldn't come to some private arrangement."

She immediately opened her purse. He shook his head.

"Oh no. Not that type of arrangement. We used to play a game

when we were younger - it's called Forfeits. And you are going to have to pay a very big forfeit."

The Missing S

Steve Barratt pulled into the yard at his normal time to find the place already open and Bob, his father, sitting ashen-faced in the office having a mug of tea. His stomach churned for a moment.

"Dad? Dad, are you OK? You look awful. Do you want to go home? I can run this place by myself for a while if you want."

"I got a phone call last night from Ted. He's on the way home. I told him I'd pick him up from London Airport. His plane comes in at half-three this afternoon. Are you coming?"

Steve nodded slowly pursing his lips, then laughed bitterly.

"So that's it, is it? I don't believe it. Eighteen months in, my dear, dear brother decides to walk out and take a year-long sabbatical leaving just the two of us to scrape by running this set-up. He spends all his money and then phones you up and says: 'Hey, Dad, I've seen the light, I've spent all my money and half of yours, can you pick me up at the airport tomorrow?' I suppose you've offered him his job back for good measure! If you want to pick him up at the airport and go all emotional, that's down to you. Don't expect me to kiss him on both cheeks and kill the fatted cow when he walks through those doors! And no, I won't be coming. You seem to forget I have a business to run."

Bob looked hurt.

"Steve, don't be bitter. He's your brother."

"God, that's rich! You haven't been reading the bloody Bible, have you? This reads like an updated version of the Prodigal Son. I remember reading about it in school."

Bob shuddered, remembering how, not only did they come to blows on that final day, but to make the split even more public, Steve had climbed up and put a large X through the last word of the sign. Instead of Barratt & Sons it now read Barratt & Son. He also amended the headed notepaper for added effect.

He gave his brother a very cool reception the following morning as he accompanied him on his travels. He was absolutely useless! Neither of them said cheerio to one another. A cursory nod sufficed. Three days later Bob gave them both their job lists. Neither son said much but as they reached the front gate, Steve then motioned to his father, who followed them out.

"You haven't seen it, have you?"

"Seen what?"

"The sign." Steve replied, motioning with his head.

The S was back in place. It now read: 'Barratt and Sons. Painters and decorators. All work undertaken.' He grimaced, closed his eyes and returned to the office saying nothing as they drove off stone faced. Early days — it would be nothing short of a miracle for the three of them to work as a team, but miracles occasionally did happen, even in the twenty-first century.

James Apps

Little Green Men

Afterwards Bowman thought that walking across the square was a mistake. It was not the sun beating down on his bare head, or the little green men standing on the paving beside a flying saucer trying to attract the attention of the crowd, but something much more distracting. Granted, the presence of the little green men was unusual, but that wasn't it.

Bowman's mistake was forgetting about the Morris Dancing Festival involving grown men and women cavorting in noisy groups bashing sticks together to the strains of some obscure folk tune played on a wheezy accordion. He should have taken to the side streets instead.

As it was, dodging one group of dancers who pranced out of a side street to join the mainstream of revellers, Bowman collided with the Fool. They were both extremely large, rotund men whose leviathan collision projected them in opposing directions with devastating effect.

Bowman and the Fool staggered into the circling maelstrom of clashing staves and prancing men scattering them every which way to crash, swearing profusely, into the rest of the dancers.

"Oy! Watch what you is doing!" Yelled an irate Morris Dancer as Bowman hurtled toward him.

Too late, Bowman the catalyst and the Fool carried the troupe across the square. The Dancers, disrupted by the rush, followed the stumbling group bent on 'having it out' with the 'lumbering oaf', resulting in a mêlée of flying sticks and angry voices.

The stick wielding tidal wave of angry dancers washed over the little green men and the flying saucer sending it rattling and banging across the cobblestones, to come to a rest against the Town Hall.

Bowman tripped over a terrified alien and crashed to the ground clutching at the soft body suddenly aware that his little town had been invaded. He and the group of confused and sorry looking green aliens came to a belly gasping stop against the bouncing spacecraft.

Gasping for breath, unable to move Bowman watched the aliens scuttle into the space craft, heard the door shut with a hiss, and felt the pressure of some sort of power, and the space craft was gone.

Seconds before somebody's Morris Staff hit his head and knocked him senseless he realised all the aliens were trying to say was 'Take me to your leader'.

Lugs's New Teddy

When the chance came, Lugs and the Ferret were on the ball. Lugs lifted the crate and carried it into the van shoving it against the rest. He shut the doors and clambered into the passenger seat as the Ferret started the engine.

A half hour later he was lifting the crates out of the van onto the floor of Big Willy's warehouse.

Big Willy's mistake was laughing when the Ferret asked for his cut. Lugs had to explain to him it was cash on the nail, which was where Lugs hung him by the collar. With their cut in the Ferret's wallet they drove off and Lugs remarked as they passed out of the gate.

"Do you fink he was upset?"

"A little."

"I suppose his mates will untie him."

"I expect so."

"We got paid all right?"

"All of it mate."

"What was it we was nicking?"

"Dunno mate, but Big Willy wanted 'em."

And that, Lugs thought, was all he needed to know.

All they had to do now was return the 'borrowed' van and go home.

Three days after the delivery Sidney the Shifter came calling with 'summink special' to show Lugs.

"It's the latest in cuddly toys, just come in. To you, half the going price. Daylight robbery mate, 'cos I knows what you likes. A genuine bargain," Sidney said.

Happy with the bargain Lugs placed it beside his bed with the rest of his Teddies, Smurfs, Rabbits and other fluffy toys.

Lugs was not the brightest penny in the box but as the Ferret's minder, and best mate, if you upset him, he was a one man walking disaster.

It was not a good idea to mess with his fluffy toys.

Watching the Ferret's favourite television program, Crime Watch, Lugs drew attention to one particular item.

"Ere, see them toys, well I got one of them," Lugs said, pointing at the screen.

"What, from Sidney the Shifter?"

And when the Ferret saw the retail price, calculated the knockdown cost and added Lugs' discount to it he snorted.

"We bin done mate. Sidney works fer Big Willy."

And Lugs sat staring at the screen for several minutes wrestling with his thoughts, eyes crossed and thumb in mouth. At last he spoke.

"I oughter bash him, boss, but if I does, he squeals and we get done."

"Right," agreed the Ferret.

"Maybe we should go and tell him we won't bash him as long as he shuts his gob," Lugs said looking pleased.

Sometimes, thought the Ferret, as they got up to pay Big Willy a visit, Lugs' profound insights can quite surprise you.

One Armed Bandits

Tonight was his lucky night, and Jolly, feeding the machines with coins knew he was on to a winner. The rows of machines, the 'one armed bandits' gleamed in the lights and as each punter pulled the lever so the machines jangled and squeaked sometimes disgorging coins, mostly not.

Jolly was, like the rest of the players, was hoping for three golds in a line, the jackpot; pure luck if it happened. Tonight Jolly felt lucky.

"Come on baby," he said, putting a coin in the slot. He pulled the lever and picked up another coin.

Morrison, the manager, watched from the observation balcony glancing occasionally at the women sitting in front of the monitors. He too felt the tension.

"Emily. I feel we may have something today," he said.

She looked up grinning. "You hope not?"

"A win on the bandits now and then keeps the punters coming," he said.

Jolly, down to his last ten coins, pulled the handle and closed his eyes.

"Come to me baby, come to me," he murmured.

His eyes snapped open when suddenly, hearing the metallic rattle of tokens, he stared unbelievingly at the line of golds.

Tokens spilled onto the floor and attendants hurried with pails taking turns filling them. Security staff kept the rest of the punters away as Jolly stood watching the tokens cascade from the mouth of the machine.

Morrison arrived smiling benignly and said: "Our cheque can cover the whole amount or you can have some in cash, many of our winners like that."

Jolly settled for a nine thousand cheque and a thousand in cash putting the cheque in a back pocket and enjoyed the feel of the bulky wad in his wallet. First stop, the pub, have a pint and then home. Instead he bought beer for a couple of friends and staggered out at closing time slightly tipsy aware of bragging about his win. Almost home a dark figure loomed in front of him.

"All right mister, hand it over," growled the dark voice.

Jolly tried resistance but a strong hand gripped him and the dark voice growled again.

"I said, hand it over chummy."

Jolly fumbled in his pocket, removed the wallet and handed it over. What happened next was odd. The hand let him go, grabbed the wallet and returning much faster as a fist that broke his nose.

He fell sprawling on the paving realising that the mugger was indeed a one - armed bandit.

On Robbery and Pussycats

Gina read the badly written note,and smiled at the nervous young man.

"You have to be kidding," she said.

"Do as you're told," he growled.

"It is incorrect to say 'I got'; you should say 'I have a gun', and money is spelt with a letter 'o'," she said.

"Look, lady, shuddup an' gimme the money," the young man snarled.

"And what do we say?"

"Just gimme the cash!"

Gina shook her head.

"Shouting will get you nowhere," she said calmly.

The gun, was one of those cheap, badly made Glock copies she used to send for scrap when she worked at the Met, a useless item really. The poor boy was shaking like a leaf; puzzled by her refusal to obey his demands.

"Come on! I ain't got all day!"

"Oh dear, I think you should calm down," she said.

"Open the till, will yer!" He almost screamed.

He was definitely panicking.

She smiled at him. "Do you like pussycats?"

He staggered, doing a double-take.

"What? Pussycats? What sort of question is that? Just gimme the cash."

"They make lovely pets. I have two. You ought to get one, it would give you something to look after and care for, and keep you calm and happy," she said aware that his hand faltered and the gun drooped limply.

"You're crazy. I hate cats," he said, startled at the sound of sirens, the noise of car doors slamming and rapidly approaching booted feet.

Gina reached across the counter, and gently, she eased the gun from his sweaty hands. He snatched at the weapon but instead faced the unwavering wrong end of the barrel aimed at his chest. Gina slipped the safety catch off, amused that the boy had omitted to activate the weapon.

"Stay very still, sonny, I know how to use one of these."

She smiled at the officers when they entered the shop, and before she handed one of them the young man's pistol, she explained.

"The silly boy was so rude, and has poor writing skills, he didn't think my customers would call 999, and has no time for pussycats. Not very bright really," she said, omitting what the officers already knew; that she was a retired firearms instructor.

Material & Environment Solutions Systems Inc. (MESSI)

Dressed like spacemen in protective suits Tommo, Davy and Sparko, third class waste recovery operatives worked the MESSI landfill facility, Brambledown Isle of Sheppey. Tommo and Davy shifted the cradle to the new spot and Sparko pushed the bucket into the pile, lifted a section of compressed garbage into the cradle. Tommo, on the hoist, lifted it onto the flat top and Davy unhooked it selecting another. The stench of rubbish, sweetened by the smell of methane gas leaking from the collectors did not bother them, but what happened next did.

Sparko operated the bucket and stopped it in mid turn.

"What's that?" he said pointing.

"Ooh er. It's a skellington," said Davy jumping back when it slipped out of the bucket and landed at his feet. "Oh, I suppose we oughter call his nibs."

His nibs called the police.

The Chief Inspector, wrinkled nose and contemptuous manner looked them up and down. "You blokes stink," he explained.

"Ours is a smelly job. It's all them pampers and stuff what people throws away," Davy said. "You gets used to it."

"Nah, I couldn't get used to a stink like that," the Inspector said.

"Yeah, but the gov'mint wants the valuable stuff and the gas," said Tommo.

"It's all about recycling," Sparko added with a grin.

The Chief Inspector, realising they had nothing to tell him let them go.

The day after the police left the pals returned to work, hungover, the familiar noise of the gas valve part of their working rhythm when suddenly Sparko's bucket loosened more clay and garbage slid down to the ground. Davy and Tommo stood gazing at the mess in amazement as Sparko withdrew the bucket.

It was filled with bones.

The cavity left in the landfill was oozing piles of bones.

"Looks like we got another bleedin' 'olidy,' said Tommo, and blew the whistle.

It happened that day the local press was bored and found that skeletons turning up at MESSI was a fascinating local story.

Before the Supervisor could hurry them away their digital cameras were redolent with pictures of piles of human bones.

The headlines declared "Mass Grave found at Brambledown" and showed pictures of Tommo, Sparko and Davy standing astonished at their find. The articles described how the three men 'in the general execution of their duties' unearthed a dozen skeletons.

For one evening at least in their local pub they were heroes and wallowed in relating the details.

"We tried to tell the coppers the first time. When all them others fell out, the papers got the story and we didn't have the heart to tell 'em," said Davy.

"They was all plastic from the 'Orspital," said Sparko.

"All part of our MESSI job," said Tommo proudly.

"It's all about recycling," said Davy.

James Apps

The Witch

Jonno and his mates passed the witch's house twice each day and ran past shouting. "Witch! Witch! Cast no spell! Or we'll send you straight to Hell!" laughing loudly when the curtains shifted and the witch herself looked out.

Shelley said the large black cat that sat in the sun on her small porch roof was her familiar.

"They have an extra teat under their armpits," Shelley said.

"What, the cat?" said Jonno.

"No dummy, the Witch. I read up on it. You don't know nothing," Shelley said, her nose wrinkling as she sniffed contemptuously. "Anyway, we don't have to worry about her because we can burn her if we want, and she knows that. They try to keep it secret and go about pretendin' to do good but underneath they is really puttin' spells on people."

Jonno had to agree with her because the Witch was always going around the place visiting old people, and making soup for folks who were ill.

What's more they had seen her feeding the stray cats in the village and catching some of them in cages.

"She eats 'em, don't she?" said Denis.

"Yeah, and makes coats and gloves outa their skins," said Colin.

"And I bet she feeds their hearts to the Devil," said Jonno, not to be outdone.

"She uses their bits in her spells. Them and the frogs, and newts and things," said Shelley.

And that was why Jonno and his mates always ran past the Witch's house on their way to and from school. Denis crossed his fingers to ward off the evil eye; Colin gripped his lucky rabbit's foot, Shelley held up a cross on a silver chain and Jonno, scared spitless, muttered 'White heather' as they ran past.

And then came the day Jonno was late coming home and had to pass the Witch's house alone. He slowed, toyed with the idea of crossing the road but instead he crossed his fingers, said: "White heather," for luck, and started his run passing the low, unkempt hedge where it joined the neighbour's fence. Racing past the gate, too late, he saw the cat on the pavement warming itself in the sun.

Jonno tripped, falling hands outstretched to break his fall, the cat underneath him. It squealed, slashed at him spitting viciously as he tried to recover.

"Ouch! You rotten ..." but at that moment he hit the gatepost and tumbled, skinning his knees, and rolled on the ground yelling in pain.

And then she was there, the Witch, her long dress swaying, her hat shading her face and hands reaching down to clutch at him.

She cackled and Jonno fainted in terror.

The End Of The World Is Nigh

The bedraggled protestor outside St James's Park underground station called out.

"Repent! The end of the world is nigh! Repent!"

His cry descended into a yell of agony when David Johns, age twenty-eight, wrenched the placard from the Doomsayer's hands and clobbered him with it.

"That for your stupid message!" He cried, menacing the terrified would-be evangelist who backed away nervously uncertain whether he should gather the remains or run away.

"But sir! The world is about to end!" he cried.

"No it isn't you bloody moron! Your mad Reverend Soon is a religious nut."

The frightened evangelist was joined by others of his group holding placards and chanting "The end of the world is nigh! Repent! Repent! The holy Reverend Soon brings the world God's message!"

"You're all loonies! There's no fiery asteroid coming to destroy the Earth. Neither is it God's vengeance on a sinful world," David said and shook a fist at the nearest placard carrier who backed away nervously.

"God is not mocked. Repent your sins and be saved!"

With that David turned away and walked off shaking his head in disbelief, and later at his desk with coffee and a task nearly completed he sat in front of the screen and listened to the latest news. There was more on the religious fanatics of the morning trip in. He read:

'... Reverend Soon of the Modern Church of Repentance urges all people to repent of their sins and ask forgiveness of God before the coming of the Punishment. The Reverend Soon, surrounded by his devoted followers in his church in Wyoming is stoically awaiting what they believe will be the end of the world at 11am their time, that is 22.00 London Time ...'

Friends tweeted amusement and happier now that everybody was taking it so lightly, he tweeted an idea.

#End of World party at my local?

His local was close to his flat in Mornington Crescent and after dinner the party was on. Mellow with drink he related his morning confrontation. He laughed loudly at the ribald comment one man made of his own experience.

"... Repent! Repent! A girl called out. I nearly did, she was a real cracker, I almost repented on the spot!"

Laughing, David checked the time and called out loudly: "Nearly time folks! Shall we count it down?"

There was a chorus of assent and led by the sober barman they began the count starting at one minute to the hour, and as they reached ten they were chanting together. The bar resounded to the counting. Five - four - three - two - one – zero ...

And the rest, was silence.

Ready Cash

Joseph agreed, the coffin did look nice. The polished wood and the brass furniture made it look luxurious, and the satin cushioning was just the right shade of pink. Joseph paid extra for a special evening viewing and even in the subdued lighting of the funeral parlour the coffin looked good.

"And sir would like hinges on the lid?"

The fawning proprietor clasped his hands together deferentially.

"Correct, with folding stays."

"And no screws or nails?"

"Totally bereft of them please."

"As sir pleases, and the matter of payment?"

"Cash on the nail of course."

The man tried to hide his disdain and nodded.

"Er we are not arranging the, er services otherwise sir?"

"No, my good fellow, we will have it delivered."

Joseph was amused to see the man wince.

"Sir is not attempting a do-it-yourself, er, funeral?"

"No, sir is not. Sir wants a coffin with a hinged lid delivered to sir's address, and sir is willing to pay for it with sir's ready cash," Joseph said, taking the amount requested from his wallet.

Mollified by the sight of the money the proprietor filled out the receipt and handed it to Joseph with the manner of one indulging an eccentric."May I ask who the casket is for sir?"

"Why, myself of course; when I am in need of it," Joseph said and smiled broadly. He left the establishment, and wrapping his voluminous coat around chuckled at the image of the poor fellow's pale, shocked face. "I must remember not to show my teeth when I do that," he muttered quietly as he strode purposely along the darkened street.

I Am Daffodil

The traffic around the island circles left and the right to disappear breathing clouds of warm vapour as it passes. I stand, mesmerised, my face warmed by the sun, a mellow, yellow glow looking out and down at the hurrying vehicles. My friends and I in green and yellow livery stand in a neat curving line, bravely facing the raging road our feet firmly in the soil, placed there involuntarily by some design greater than ours. My neighbours say that being somewhere and greeting the sunshine in the Spring is enough. I am sure that like me, they would rather be in a quiet orchard, under the trees where the sun dapples the grass and birds sing happily.

I like to hear the insects buzzing, see birds flitting around and small animals hopping close by eating the grass, and hear the trees waking from their winter sleep. Like us they lay dormant, waiting for the spring. Sometimes, so I was told, you can hear the sap rushing upwards giving life to the leaves and blossom which brings the bees.

And now, even with the noise of the traffic I hear a buzzing, hovering bee. I feel the vibrations of the air close beside me, the touch of hard feet, the buzz of busy wings and feel the weight drop on to petals inside and wait in anticipation.

It comes, the probing touch as the creature hovers inside close to my delicate centre. The bee sucks the light nectar, the divine fluid I exude to call it to me, and I feel its soft body touch gently and feel the rubbing - an exchange of precious pollen.

It is later I feel the exquisite energy flow down my stem, touch the base under the soil and add its fertile substance to mine. I sigh with pleasure and hear other friends close by sighing in happiness as they too experience this wonderful orgiastic treat, this love fest shared along the curving golden row; a sigh heard even above the noisy traffic.

And was that an acknowledgement of the procreative orgy or was it the cool wind that moved us for a moment to rustle gently, our heads waving like the golden host of the poet's evocative words?

The Purity Pledge

Like most of the boys in his church youth club Barry found Deanna attractive. Her long dark hair, her cat-like elegance, her alluring presence and that she was small and pretty added to her fascination. She used make-up to accentuate her delicate features and creamy pale skin, white teeth and red lips. During prayers he managed to catch her glance and smiled at her. When she returned his smile he felt a sudden, trembling thrill that stirred thoughts of carnal desire.

A sin because, like all the others in his church youth group he had signed up to a purity pledge. When, after prayers, she crossed the room to meet him he didn't feel like remaining a pledger.

"You are Barry?" she said as she came to a graceful halt.

"Er, yes, and you are Deanne, I er, oh, hello," he said.

She giggled.

"Why don't you talk to me?" she said seductively.

He felt a shudder of excitement and said: "I tried to but wasn't sure what you would do."

"I won't eat you," she said taking his hand in hers.

"I should walk you home this evening," he said.

Her eyes seemed to flash and he felt a warm, inner glow. "Yes, yes, of course you must," she said and kissed his cheek.

Walking to her house hand in hand she listened attentively and now and then they kissed, she guiding his fumbling hands with familiar skill and all thoughts of purity pledges disappeared from Barry's Christian mind.

"And you, what about you?" he asked.

"Oh, I live alone, my people are dead," she said.

Her house was shaded by pollarded Limes and under an arched porch was a plain wooden door which she quickly unlocked.

"Er, do you realise I have no idea how to get home from here," he said.

"Oh, come in, I'll show you," she said.

The dimly lit interior revealed a black and red décor with curtains instead of internal doors, and a pervading aroma of incense.

"You're a Goth, right?"

"If you like," she said, and put her arms around him.

This time there was no holding back and all thoughts of purity pledges disappeared from Barry's mind as he gladly lost his virginity.

"I should go home," he said afterwards.

She snuggled close, and standing, took his hand pulling him easily from the settee and smiled.

"Why don't you stay?"

Lost in desire he followed her as she pushed aside the bedroom curtain. Holding his hand firmly she drew him further into the room. For a brief moment he resisted wanting to run when he saw the dread thing resting on the floor but her delicate hands held him tightly preventing his escape.

"A coffin! What are you?"

"Don't you know?" she said, laughing softly.

His question was answered when her sharp teeth bit into his throat.

James Apps

A Walk through the Park

The girl turned into the park needing no guiding light to see her way, familiar with the route. Tossing her dark hair back as she pulled her mobile out of her cut downs' pocket and stabbed the keyboard with her thumbs, giggling at the replies. Some of her friends thought she was chancing things walking the park late at night. She had laughed refusing an escort of two of the boys.

"I really don't need them," she said.

Three men watched the girl walk confidently onto the paving her shoes tapping softly on the bitumen and moved softly and yet quickly to intercept her. This girl who was stupidly walking on her own through the park dressed in skimpy clothing was a target. Asking for it, they said.

"We won't have much trouble with this one," whispered Jerry. Don and Adam gave a low, predatory chuckle moving through the shadows until they were ahead of her. It was too easy.

She didn't see the men until they grabbed her and hauled her into the bushes, her clothes snagging on small branches, one shoe flying off to land in the grass and her mobile bouncing away on the path.

"Got her," Jerry said, chuckling as Don and Adam throwing her on her back under the bushes tore at her clothes stripping the fabric from her body to expose her breasts and legs.

"Me first," Jerry said, already unzipping his jeans.

The girl, her face now free of a restricting, rough skinned hand opened her mouth as if to scream. Her small tongue and perfect white teeth caught the spill over light from the street lamps some forty metres away on the paving, and she chuckled softly deep in her throat licking her lower lip with her tongue.

"Yes," she said. "You first."

And then began the terror.

~~~

The story Inspector Simon Ward gleaned from Henky the frightened dosser confirmed what Jean Sampson, his forensic officer had suggested.

"You saw a girl? Describe her please."

"She was skinny, pretty, small with dark hair. She comes into the

56

park and I watches the blokes go after her, and then I hears screaming, so I stays where I was." Henky said, nervously.

"Do you know the men?"

Henky evaded the Inspector's gaze. "Nah Inspector, I dunno who they are."

Inspector Ward, reluctant to return to the marquee shuddered.

Torn clothing soaked in blood and multiple wounds; he could handle that.

But the torn throat, popped out eyeballs, the great gash in the chest: that he couldn't handle.

And even worse than all that was the finger marks on the pallid throats, and the footprints in the grass, one a small bare foot and the other a woman's shoe.

Inspector Ward knew that the killer of three grown men was a dark haired girl who was not afraid to walk alone in the dark.

James Apps

Opposition

I heard a man say that black was the opposite of white, and darkness was the absence of light. I heard the same man say that night was the opposite of day, and wet was the opposite to dry. He seemed upset, when in opposition to his remarks, I questioned his reasons why. Of course, he said, black is no colour at all, and white is all the colours that be, and without light one cannot see. With contempt, he explained to me why that which is wet cannot possibly be dry. And so, I at once, said to this bipolar dunce, that black, given the right surface, reflects the brightest of hues, and white without relief makes the eyes confused. The eye has no source but darkness, so is the claim, yet when beheld by a lover's gaze shines bright as any flame. Ah, said he, you cannot deny that, that which is wet cannot be dry. Not so, I replied, when you think of your body, within, are the fluids contained by your impermeable skin.

~~~

And yet, with tones as cutting as a knife, he said, you cannot deny the opposite of death is life. Nor the opposite of go is stop, or that the only way is down when you reach the top. And even, with words so dull, that the antithesis of empty must of course be full? So, I said, that even on the carnal meat, some creature, for its nourishment must therefore eat. If he should also stand still as a tree for a single day, he would still be rushing around the sun; and by the way, could he tell the place on any sphere where day and night begins, or which season of the day has wings. As for standing on the highest point there is no call to move anywhere at all, unless of course you mean you cannot choose a place somewhere in between? In reply to your final surmise, do you think that it is wise, to question why empty space can be such a crowded place.

The Man with the Wooden Leg

The man with the wooden leg stumped up the hill stopping occasionally to rest. He leaned on his walking stick glad of the support and wishing the hill was not so steep. He was nearly at the top and glad of it when he saw his destination. The wooden leg was a hindrance and although the stick helped, his journey from the village below was slow especially when he had to be careful of his footing on the slippery surface. He nearly slipped on the turn into the gate but managed to keep his balance with the aid of the stick.

Reaching the door he rang the bell.

The woman answered looking pleased.

"Your husband's new leg," he said, handing her the parcel.

James Apps

I likes to sit

I likes to sit in the armchair set in the bay window and look down at the street. It's funny what goes on down there.

It used to be that people walked to work or school. It used to be kids riding their bikes and the mothers with the littl'uns dragging them along by hand or stuck in a buggy with bags dangling from the handles.

You don't see many nowadays.

They gets in their cars and shuffle for parking spaces.

Me, well I sits in me chair watchin' 'em.

I sips me tea with a little totty in it to help it taste better and sees 'em all.

I sleeps when I wants to and sometimes I watches, dozing off in me chair, and now and then to wake up and see what I can see. I sees all sorts, especially the girls and their boyfriends but I tells nobody. None of my business what they does in their cars. All I had when I was their age was the alleyways and the bushes.

Just sitting in my armchair watching.

But that's not what I'm talking about.

Just about a quarter after three last night I looks out the window and sees it. Two men come out of number forty three humping something heavy down the steps. One man rested the lump on the bins beside the gate. The other one unlocked a car and lifted the boot lid.

I thought, aye, aye, something's fishy here.

With the boot lid up both men carried the lump out the gate and stuffed it in the boot.

It was then I sees the foot dangling from the wrappings.

I didn't do nothing about what I sees.

None of my business.

But just in case, I takes their car number I wonder if they knows about the shoe what dropped into the gutter when they drove off?

Peter Apps

Shadows

The shadows were advancing again and his pulse quickened. He did not believe in ghosts, so he assumed they were human. It was getting worse, every night he saw the shadows among the trees and bushes in his garden but who were they?

His best guess was that they were local kids, daring each other to explore the reclusive old man's garden or even get a glimpse of him but all he saw were shadows. When he had first got out of prison, he had still been in shock at what he had done. He still found it difficult to sit still and spent his days cleaning and tidying the house, and keeping the garden in pristine condition. Never satisfied, never able to relax once one room was tidy then the next needed decorating or a flower bed needed replanting. At night the screams of the children, trapped in the burning mini-bus filled his nightmares.

He stayed, trapped behind the high garden fence, unable to face anyone; without a phone because he could not bear to talk to anyone. He did not have a radio or a television because every scene seemed to remind him of his drunken stupidity at the wheel of a tanker full of petrol.

For a long time the shadows were just that, strange shapes created by the few lights reaching the garden and the wind, but he was older now. Maybe his eyesight was failing and they really were just shadows but whatever he thought about ghosts and things going bump in the night, they seemed to creep across the lawn getting closer to the house.

That night he stared in horror as a shadow was cast across his window.

It was lucky for the rescue workers that his body was found the next day, spotted by the postman, the only person to regularly visit. Without the sharp-eyed postman his body could have lain there for months, steadily rotting away.

The coroner declared that it was death by natural causes, following a massive stroke but the paramedics who first attended, never forgot the look of terror that seemed to distort his face, neither could they forget his hands. Although there was not a mark on him, the body reminded them of someone who had been trapped in a terrible fire.

Power Cut

Fortunately terrorist groups are as stupid and as those who claim to defend us. Maybe terror attacks are intended to cow the enemy into submission but a terrified animal is hardly logical and just lashes out. People seek vengeance.

The attack on the Twin Towers in New York was certainly a grand gesture but did it achieve anything? Certainly it shocked people all around the world, planes were briefly grounded but the effects did not last. Effectively, it took the lives of a dozen highly trained operatives, hours of planning and a great deal of luck to achieve a blip. My aim was for something more lasting.

For myself I'm content to live in a village without CCTV cameras everywhere, I do not have a driving license or any other ID with my picture on it. I have never been caught by the law so my fingerprints are not on file.

I know a little about disguise, enough to confuse facial recognition software and I live near towns and cities where there's high unemployment and riots have occurred. In short, I have recruited twenty or so helpers from where disaffected folk gather. It seems that those twenty have spoken to others in their turn but I do not ask.

I do have a laptop but I only use it near a pub in town where I hacked the Wi-Fi network ages ago. I use it to update my gardening website about the growing of parsnips. I could not think of a more boring subject and the few visitors seldom stay. My group knows of the hidden page where I pass on instructions. There's more, codes and the like but I'm not giving you the details yet.

My search for recruits led me to suppliers for the explosives I needed, namely C4 shaped charges. Other materials, thin copper wire and fireworks are easily obtainable.

The campaign has only been going on for a week now and the effects are mounting. One electrical pylon failing means electrical supplies being rerouted. We scored ten successful hits with shaped charges and that means power failures. Thin copper wire tied to a firework rocket can touch power cables, shorting them out. Sometimes it just produces spectacular sparks, sometimes enough of an arc to trip breakers and sometimes the heat can melt part of the cable and dozens can be let off in one night.

My aim might have been simple, to destroy the electricity network so that the economy could not function but I had not bargained on my group enjoying their work so much. Spectacular fireworks, pylons crashing down are just too exciting even though three were shot last night.

My solar-panels and diesel-generator keeps me supplied so I watch news of copycat attacks across North America and Europe with growing alarm. What is worse, half of the country suffered a blackout yesterday and at least a quarter is still without power while new blackouts are occurring today. I may have gone too far.

The Anniversary

Joe ducked as the shadow flashed across his eyes and the roar of the engine deafened him. Then there was nothing except for the image of a wartime aircraft flying impossibly low burnt into his brain.

What was real was the screech of brakes and him being thrown onto the bonnet of a car. Luckily the car had nearly stopped so the impact was far less serious than it could have been. The driver leapt out, yelling, "Oh Christ! Oh Christ!"

As Joe gathered his wits and struggled to his feet, 'Oh Christ' became an angry, "What the f—k were you playing at?"

"You didn't see it?" Joe asked.

"See what? You just jumped sideways and doubled over."

"There was this plane, a Spitfire, I think. It was so low the propeller could have taken my head off. Didn't you see…"

He trailed off. Tall trees bounded the road, a plane could not have flown so low. Joe was fully recovered by then and the driver was torn between relief and anger at being so badly frightened.

The anger won.

"If you're seeing things like that then you want to lay off the vino, mate." he snapped as he leapt into his car and drove off.

Although physically unharmed, Joe was badly shaken and scared. He knew that it was the Anniversary but did seventy-five years have any mystical significance? He did not think so and his father had died on the thirty-seventh anniversary. Joe was not superstitious, certainly not in the way that his father had been. He assumed that his father had died because superstitious dread of the Anniversary had aggravated his heart condition.

Modern medicine controlled his own, inherited heart condition and curses did not exist. He thought differently now and he hurried home, locking the door behind him as he sought safety.

He poured himself a stiff drink and considered what he knew of the Anniversary. Joe's great-grandfather had become attracted to his best friend's fiancée and the deep friendship between the two pilots turned into bitter hatred. When the groom-to-be got into difficulties over France, it was suggested that Joe's great-grandfather held back and allowed him to be shot down and killed. Nothing was ever proved, and in the heat of the dog-fight Joe's great-grandfather could have spotted another enemy aircraft but no-one really believed it. Others were reluctant to fly with him and he was transferred to a training squadron as an instructor.

The Anniversary was a few days after that incident. The fiancée was fatally wounded in a bombing raid. Before she finally lost consciousness, all her emotion was directed at cursing Joe's great-grandfather. She and her fiancé had been due to be married the day after the dog-fight and would have been away on honeymoon.

Joe would have to check the death certificates of his great-grandfather and grandfather. A ghostly curse or just plain fear, it did not matter for if they died on the Anniversary, then it was his turn.

Peter Apps

Dilemma

He stood watching the old biddies coming out of the post office some still holding their pensions in their hands. It should be easy if he timed it right, he could grab the bag or the cash without even breaking his stride as he ran past.

He knew that it was wrong but what would his dad say?

"It's them or us son. Besides I bet there's a whip round for the old dear before you're round the corner."

That's how he thought, putting his family first and the rest of the world nowhere, them or us fashion. At least that is how he would think when he was sober. When he was drunk even his family was against him and needed to be put it in its place. The boy rubbed his bruised ear wondering if the hearing would ever return. That blow from his father had been the last straw and he had run. Now he was hungry and desperate, unable to seek help for, despite his hatred for his father, it was his example that still dominated, but now it was them or me.

Still his conscience made him hesitate until it occurred to him that the pensioners were all done, hurrying off to the shops to spend their money. It was business types now with handfuls of letters and parcels to be sent.

He almost felt relieved except that he faced another day without food unless he tried begging again. It was pointless hanging around the post office now, he may as well sit in the library for a while and get warm. He shuffled off, depressed and without hope, turning into a deserted road.

Ahead of him, one of the pensioners he had seen, tripped to fall sprawling on the pavement. Her bag flew wide and her purse tumbled from it to lie amongst the food she had bought. No one else had seen the incident and she was obviously shocked or stunned.

The boy stared hungrily at the loaf of bread and the packet of ham lying beside the purse, he only had to bend forwards. It was almost too tempting but he still possessed a gentleness that his father had not completely beaten out of him. His instinct was still to help. The old lady groaned. Although it had seemed like hours of indecision it had been less than a second but one way or the another, he had to act. He bent down, stretching out his hand ...

Taming The Monster

The man wearily shuffled down the corridor. It seemed as if the fight had gone on for ever and he was exhausted. He reached the door, the final barrier. Beyond was the monster, lurking in his lair.

Even as he pushed the door open, he smelt the stench of rotting food prevalent amongst the other malodorous, foetid smells of decaying life. There was little light. Some filtered through heavy curtains and the man was tempted to make his way across the dark cavern to throw them open but delays were dangerous.

At any moment the monster could wake while the man felt his way through the foul, indescribable filth that made up the floor but it remained asleep, unaware that its lair had been invaded.

The man knew what he had to do. Only the mantra he had rehearsed over and over on his long trek to the lair would tame the beast. If only he could repeat it with the power and strength to penetrate the monster's soul.

The beast was stirring but not yet alert. The man leant forward gripping the monster's shoulders. Startled, it stared at the man.

This was the moment, the beast was trapped, entranced by the man's eyes boring into his own.

There would never be a better chance to recite the spell.

"David, this room is a tip. If it's not tidied up by lunchtime you'll be grounded for a week and you'll lose your pocket money for a month."

Peter Apps

Everything's Fine Dear

The scene is a back garden with the slightly dotty lady of the house talking to her husband on a mobile phone. Her husband greets her and she replies:-

Hello dear. How did the orientation day go?
(pause)
That's good. And you're all ready for the interview? I'm sure you'll get the job.
(pause)
Me? Everything's fine here. I don't know what you mean by that tone in my voice
(pause)
Well all right then. The front garden wall collapsed. It's nothing. I can sort it out. You worry about the interview.
(pause)
I'll get a builder around as soon as possible. I'll get quotes for the front lawn at the same time. Concentrate on the interview.
(pause)
No silly. A few bricks haven't ruined the lawn. It's the tyre tracks.
(pause)
The tracks from the lorry that knocked the wall down. Don't worry about it. Are you still preparing for your interview?
(pause)
No, I won't be able to pick you up tomorrow. The car needs a new windscreen. It'll have to be replaced before I can drive it.
(pause)
Some bricks fell on it. Don't worry. I'll call the windscreen people as soon they're able to get to the car.
(pause)
They've already pulled the lorry back. The car got a couple of dents but it doesn't look too bad.
(pause)
No. The breakdown people can't touch it until the builders say they can.

(pause)
It was pushed a little way into the living room and they want to check the wall before the car's moved.
(pause)
Calm down dear. You'll fail the interview if you let yourself get upset.
(pause)
They'll move the car just as soon as they get those jack things in place. Once the upstairs stops resting on it they'll be able to pull it out.
(pause)
Oh don't be so melodramatic. Of course the house isn't going to fall down. They're not even sure that they'll have to pull it down.
(pause)
Please calm down. Screaming like that is not going to help. With the house insurance and the compensation everything will be fine.
(pause)
You said that you were going to renew it. It was the night I dropped your wallet in the waste disposal unit. You were upset then but you definitely said that you wanted to be sure that it was done right.
(pause)
They did say that the lorry was stolen so it wasn't insured. Is that going to be a problem, dear?
(pause)
All you have to do is calm down and do well in the interview tomorrow. We'll be all right with the extra money and we'll have to move for your new job anyway. It won't be so bad.
(pause)
No it's not the last straw and I'm not discussing a divorce while you're in this state. Call me back after the interview and you've got the job.

Peter Apps

Reminiscing

I was a teenager, strolling along the seafront not far from where Sheppey FM is now. Looking across the Thames Estuary, the nearest channel leads round to the River Medway and ships travelled to and fro all the time so it was nothing unusual to see two sets of lights converging. It was too dark to make out the ships; it was a winters night and dark almost before I had got out of school but it did not matter, there was nothing unusual.

It was the metallic clang got my attention. It was not loud but it was certainly unusual. Glancing out to sea, the lights had stopped and were a confused mess but I could not pick out any detail.

I was hungry by then and anyway, how serious could a single blow be? It now all seemed so normal so, as youngsters tend to do, I went home for tea.

That evening I caught the local news. At the time, local TV or radio meant SE England, not the local community it is now, so it was something of a shock to discover that my clang had made the TV and the next day the National media.

It turned out that two ships had collided, one had sunk and one a crew member had been killed. I can't remember many of the details now but it still makes me think. After all, I had witnessed a terrible disaster and not even realised it.

Leave 'em Laughing

Hello Dr. Jorgansen, this is Professor Williams here. I've just noticed a blue corona around your laboratory. I was wondering, does your research have anything to do with time travel?

(Pause)

No, I have not rung up to laugh at your crackpot theories. It's just that...

(Pause)

No, I'm not preparing to sell some scurrilous story to the press. It's just that...

(Pause)

Doctor, I'm a professor of mediaeval history so I'm not in a position to debunk your theories. On the contrary I have reason to think that you've made a breakthrough.

(Pause)

I can hear the sirens as well and I certainly did not call the police just to harass you. I'm not surprised that someone did though. It's just that...

(Pause)

Dr. Jorgansen will you please stop interrupting me. This unscientific, bookwormy interfering old professor, as you so nicely put it, rang you to offer his congratulations. You see, I'm on the fifth floor of the main building and there's this ruddy great dinosaur peering in.

Anthony Padman

A Time To Say Goodbye

Ben was my very best friend. We cycled to school together and back. When one of us was without his the other gave him a lift, carrying him on the crossbar. In class we sat next to each other. I was not much good at Trigonometry having jumped two forms (the teachers said I was clever to be placed with Ben) so I depended very much upon him helping me. He was brilliant at everything. Mathematics, English, English Literature – the lot.

One day Ben fell seriously ill. He could not attend school. Well, not just for one day or two but weeks on end. I missed him terribly. All seven of us in the class were preparing for the final school leaving examinations. Our teacher simply told us Ben was in hospital undergoing a serious operation.

One Friday after school, plucking up courage, I rode my bicycle to the hospital. I was allowed to see Ben. He was in a room of his own. His mother sat in a corner watching him. His eyes were closed. He looked pale. Over his midriff there was a thick roll of bandages where they had operated on him.

Ben must have sensed my presence because he slowly opened his eyes to see me. He smiled. I said nothing but moved towards him. I took hold of his hand. Ben knew all what I wanted to say. I could feel it in the warmth of his hand.

Within a few minutes a big lady in uniform wearing a blue belt with a silver buckle entered the room. A small watch clipped to her top left pocket hung upside down. She looked at me. It meantI must leave. I stroked Ben's hand as I disengaged mine from his and went to sit on a chair next to Ben's mother.

The big lady spent quite a while attending to Ben. Then she came over to me. Her motherly face was soft and gentle. We went out of the room and she spoke to me. Oh! Ben I was so sorry!

On Monday, our teacher, who had a wonderful gift for words, asked us all to stand as he led prayers for Ben. We were all hoping for his miraculous recovery. It was a solemn occasion.

The following Wednesday our teacher gave us the dreaded news. Ben had passed away. It was the saddest day in my life.

"Boys," he said, "There is something I want to tell you. Ben's mother wishes to thank each one of you for thinking of her son. Just before Ben died he told his mother he had seen you all standing around him and he was able to say goodbye. She is grateful that you were with him. Now bow your heads."

Some four decades have gone by since. And I would not have given this much thought but for the fact that Ben was not a even Christian. You see, he was a Buddhist.

Anthony Padman

A Rose By Any Name

Sometimes I wonder about the career of Pastor Manfred von Hennig.

He was at the pinnacle of his career, and professor of Tropical Medicine at the University of Auerstadt when it happened. Surely, he thought, nothing could disrupt this perfect idyll!

Then came the war.

The Professor was too valuable to be inducted into the forces. But, Dieter, his eighteen-year son was conscripted and trained for the brand new panzers being produced. Throughout his nine months of training, Dieter was granted only one furlough. The family treasured this get-together.

Came July, 1943: The Army permitted Dieter one letter to his parents – his regiment was going to the Caucasus. The general consensus at home was that a vastly superior enemy was now repulsing the German Home Forces.

Christmas was bleak. The winter was the worst in memory. Snowploughs had to cut passages through ten-foot drifts for military transport. Their close friends were unable to visit them. Making the best of the situation, they stayed at home celebrating Yuletide by themselves. Sylvester morning, Frau Hennig got up to place a red rose in the vase on Dieter's desk. Then, whispering a prayer for him, she had withdrawn from his room. She had done this every day since he left.

The front-door bell rang about three in the afternoon. The Professor opened the door. There were two men wearing full military uniform. He led them up to his apartment. The officers had important post from army headquarters. Opening their leather briefcase they handed over a letter and a small parcel. Then clicking their heels they saluted and left.

The letter had a black border. The Professor read the letter silently:

I have to inform you with deep regret that your son Unter-Offizier Dieter von Hennig was killed in the tank battle at Kursk. He died a true soldier.

It was signed by an Army General.

74

He sat next to his wife holding her hand. Gently, he placed the letter on her lap. He opened the parcel. It contained Dieter's penknife, a fountain pen and a letter in an unsealed envelope. He took it out. It had obviously been written in great haste. Again, the Professor read it but this time aloud:

Dearest Mother and Father,

I have only a few minutes. We are to spearhead a panzer attack. The enemy is threatening to encircle us; he is strong with endless reserves.

If I don't come back, I want you to know how much I love you. Mother, you always put a fresh flower in my room. My favourite was the white rose from your garden.

Always,

Your son, Dieter.

That night the professor and his wife went into Dieter's room. As they entered they were attracted by the scent of a newly plucked rose. They switched on the light. Astounded, they found the red flower in the vase had changed colour - into a fresh, WHITE rose.

In 1949 Manfred von Hennig decided to enter the Church. That's where I met him.

And Where's My Share

It is often said that medical students are notorious for their irreverence to cadavers they have to dissect whilst doing their training. They could of course be harmless roguish pranks! Sometimes the intended joke miscarries. All hell is then let loose.

This is a tale often repeated as true. I suppose it has a ring of truth.

A group of medical students were together after a session on the dissecting table. Over their drinks the conversation shifted to spirits and ghosts which were acknowledged to inhabit the mortuary.

Three among the five moving the conversation along were aware that the youngest of their colleagues was sensitive to such suggestions. Ashamed he might be exposed as a believer, with an air of bravado he burst out, "You really believe in these things? I don't."

The leader of the group waited till the import of what had been just said had fully sunk in.

"Are you then saying there cannot be ghosts and spirits haunting the mortuary? Why do you think none of the staff ever go in there alone?" Why, even the senior medical personnel won't venture in there alone! You think all that is tosh, sentimental rubbish?"

The young student knew he had been ensnared. To deny meant loss of face! No, he had to go through with it. "Yes, pure sentimental rubbish!" he added

"Right, listen chaps, we'll see if this youngster's heart is as big as his mouth. This is what we'll do. There are five new cadavers in the mortuary laid out under sheets on separate tables. Here are five cubes of sugar you can have. Go to the mortuary at dead of night and place one cube in the right hand of each of the bodies. We'll certainly know by the morning if you were fearless."

With that he wrapped up the five cubes of sugar in plain white tissue-paper and handed them over to the young student!

Nigh on midnight, the youngster made his way to the mortuary. A single bulb lit the pathway to the door. He knew an arrangement had been made for the door to be left unlocked. It was very cold inside. Not expecting anything untoward he made his way past one cadaver and the next, lifting up the right edge of every covering sheet and leaving one cube of sugar as a mark of his presence.

Then it was time to leave. But a noise attracted his attention. He turned to look. A sixth cadaver he had overlooked was sitting up, its torso still covered by the white sheet. In a hellish voice it demanded, "And where is mine?"

The young student fled shrieking as if the hounds of hell were after him!

There is nothing more left to tell save that in the aftermath one mad medical student had to be committed to the local lunatic asylum. And an irate faculty of medical inspectors spent over a year before deciding they were unable to reach any conclusion.

Pelandok

The Pelandok is a very small mouse-like deer found in the jungles of Malaysia. Its technical English name is Chevrotain but the Malays call it Pelandok. Rarely seen save in its habitat, some natives regard it as a great delicacy!

Among the creatures in the forest the Pelandok is credited with having the best brains and being the most intelligent of them all. The stories of Pelandok using his wits to escape from his captors are legion and many a child's evening has been spent by listening to them.

Here is one.

Father Pelandok was out one day foraging. He had to be careful because he was so small. There were dangers around every corner in the forest. With an unusually dry spell of weather lately he found he could hop over today onto a small piece of land which would normally be surrounded by water. As he had guessed food was plentiful there so he could eat to his heart's content. Then with the hot sun shining down upon him, he dug a small hole and went to sleep.

Unfortunately, he slept too soundly. When he woke up it was to the sound of lashing rain, roaring thunder and blue flashes of lightning. The monsoons had broken a bit too early and rainwaters had already risen surrounding him completely on his island cutting him off from the mainland. The rains continued for another five days and by now Father Pelandok realised he was truly marooned. The waters kept rising and soon he had to withdraw for safety to much higher ground.

Every day when he went down for a drink, he saw a beady-eyed crocodile watching him – with tears in its eyes – not because he pitied Pelandok but because he relished instead the tasty meal he would make. Pelandok senior thought out a plan.

"Hey, crocodile", he said, "Are they many of you in these waters?"

"Of course, there are hundreds of us waiting to play with friends like you."

"I bet there are not enough to make a line from here to the mainland," continued Pelandok.

"I bet you there are," said the crocodile. "Shall I prove that to you tomorrow? Then will you come down to me in the water?"

"All right, I promise."

But the Pelandok had no intention of becoming a meal for the crocodile.

The next day when Pelandok came down to the water he saw a long line of crocodiles, nose to tail, stretching right back to the mainland.

"Now, let me count how many of you there are," Father Pelandok assured the first crocodile "before we start becoming friends."

"Yes, but be quick about it," said the unsuspecting crocodile.

Keeping safely away from the jaws of the crocodile, Pelandok jumped on the back of the first one counting loudly as he raced towards the mainland. Once he was home on the mainland he simply disappeared.

The crocodiles now realised they had been duped. However, it was too late.

Anthony Padman

The Little Corporal

The young soldier was twenty-three years old. He had been in uniform since eighteen but he was already a veteran campaigner. Here, more than a thousand miles distant he was so far away from his fiancée Nancy! They should have been wedded by now and if the Lord willed it, a father probably of two children! His eyes turned misty.

In the mountain passes of Italy he was holding the front line. There had been no reinforcements since his regiment left home. The soldiers were grumbling. His own officers had lost heart. The enemy, over one hundred thousand strong, was waiting to pounce, annihilate them.

Unbelievably there came a bit of good news. The French Directory had appointed a new Commanding General. He sounded foreign. The soldier did not know nor had he heard of his name.

His own regimental commander had read out the proclamation issued by the new general. He guaranteed final victory. He urged the French soldier to follow him without question, fight the battles he planned and they would see themselves on the rich plains of Lombardy, the most beautiful in all Italy. The French Army of Italy, had been jeered at by their enemy but within the year it was the enemy troops that were prisoners or dead.

At the command post, battle-scarred Generals could barely restrain themselves. Before them was their 26 year old Commander-in-Chief, barely 5'3" tall, pale, emaciated and looking like he still needed his first shave. But his voice and personality over-bore them. His words were of fire and there was steel in his determination. This was a General to be obeyed!

Within five days of taking command the new general had fought four battles in the mountains, defeating the enemy every time. He split the armies of Sardinia and Austria persuading the King of Sardinia to plead for terms.

Marcel was overjoyed. Soon he may be going home.

That winter night was bitterly cold. The soldier manning the frontier moved closed to the fire. Beyond him lay another new Austrian army over 100,000 strong. He had been warned to be vigilant.

80

There was a clatter of hooves and a senior general officer rode into his post. He lost no time checking the dispositions of the French forces, then dismounted warming himself before the fire. The soldier took out a crust of bread. He shared it with his General. The General turned over inside his cloak and went to sleep. Marcel guarded him.

One decade later the same soldier was in Belgium with his regiment waiting to be reviewed by the French Emperor.

"Sire," he shouted, "Before the Battle of Bassano, I shared with you my last crust of bread. I now ask of you bread for my father worn down with age and poverty." The Emperor halted the review. He immediately settled a generous pension upon the father and made Marcel a Captain.

Such are the facts of legend.

Le Petit Sergent

Twelve months ago he was an unknown in the French Army living in a garret. Now at 27 years he had the imperial families of Europe at his feet.

Victorious in every battle, he had savaged four Austrian armies each 100,000 strong relying upon his same battered French troops, at best never more than 40,000 men. In between, he had cowed the forces of the Doge, the Pope and the Italian Princes and trounced the royal armies of Sardinia and Sicily. At twenty seven he had settled himself in the Ducal Palace at Milan to resolve all outstanding matters concerning the European States Republican France had liberated, seemingly exercising plenipotentiary powers. The Austrian delegates threatened him once with their allies Prussia and Russia – Napoleon took out a porcelain vase and smashed it on the floor. "I can destroy your monarchy within 3 months like that vase if I wished it," and left them. He dispatched a message to the Austrian commander his army will be marching against Austria. Accept hostilities within twenty-four hours. The Austrians promptly signed the *Campo Formio* treaty.

Napoleon could have become the world's richest man. The wealth of Europe was his to take. Delegates offered millions in gold to influence him, without success. The Emperor of Austria promised a new kingdom for the General to rule in perpetuity. His restless mind was already on other important projects, like boring a tunnel through the Simplon Pass, and of stopping Britain's expansion by attacking her colonies – and with Egypt as the primary objective.

He was fearless in battle. In forcing the British from Toulon he personally led the charge. An English bayonet thrust reminded him of that until his death. He had a premonition about his future. He confided to Letitia long before he had created her the Queen-Mother of one French Emperor and three European Kings that if he were not dead on the field by twenty-one he was destined for great things.

The Austrian military control of Italy lay around three fortified towns. They controlled the approaches to these with murderous firepower. These had to be taken:

The battle was long and bloody. The Austrians were routed.

The French launched a night attack. Shouting, "Follow your General," Napoleon threw himself into the fray. Lodi fell.

The battle raged two days and nights. Napoleon was in the thick of it. Twice his horse was killed under him. He was flung into the bog. A grenadier of the old guard dragged him out and sheltered him behind his body. "Mon petit Sergent, you win our battles – we'll do the fighting."

Thus the world's greatest soldier-statesman became better known to his soldiers as "Le Petit Sergent"

Ruth Partis

Night-Time At The Movies

Peter looked as tired as he felt. He moaned to everyone in the pub but they weren't sympathetic. Trouble was, Peter had a lot on his mind, especially when he was trying to sleep.

His car was old and unreliable: his job was demanding, and tedious: his children were still a strain on his resources: and his wife – well she shopped. And she snored.

The barmaid asked if he'd tried counting sheep, he had, but the thought of roast lamb had given him indigestion.

A stranger spoke 'You could try what I do. I give my brain something intense but un-important to do.

'Like what?' said Peter impatiently.

'Well you could do multiplication sums in your head, or keep doubling numbers.'

Peter sighed. He wasn't very good at numbers.

'What I do' he continued 'Is go through the alphabet thinking of films with one word titles.'

Peter thought that he was quite mad, but that night when he'd been in bed wide awake for an hour, listening to the clock ticking and his wife snoring, he thought he'd give it a go.

It was easy to start with, Aliens, Braveheart and Cabaret, but he was stuck on D until he remembered Dracula, From the back of his brain came Exodus a film he'd seen as a youngster and then he thought of his granddaughters, in the car belting out 'Let it Go' from Frozen.

G was easy, the pottery scene from Ghost was unforgettable and took his mind right off his credit card bill.

H took him a while, then he suddenly remembered 'Help' the very silly Beatles film.

I was easy. Iris was his mother's name.

And J, well who could forget Robin Williams in Jumanji.

He was aware that he was still wide awake.

K was a problem, but then he remembered Jane Fonda in Klute. He hoped it was spelt with a K.

Then there was Lolita, Moonstruck and Network. He was well aware that he was remembering the women in films rather than the films. His tummy rumbled which reminded him of 'Food Glorious Food' from Oliver. His mind strayed briefly to children's films and he quickly added Pinocchio and Ratatouille.

Then he realised he'd forgotten Q and was stuck. Eventually thought of Quadrophenia. Thinking of the violence in that quickly took him to Scarface and Trainspotting.

Trying to find one for U almost had him out of bed in desperation to look on the computer but then he remembered Ulysses, a film he'd never seen. Then he remembered that he'd dragged his reluctant wife to see Videodrome, They'd watched Waterworld together too, and hated them both.

He didn't think it mattered, as it was all in his head, that he had to cheat himself for X-men and then it took him ages to remember Barbara Streisand in Yentle.

He spent a long time trying to think of Z but amazingly just as he remembered Zulu he went off to sleep zzzzzzzzzzzzzzz.

The Sad Story of James Andrew O'Rouke

James Andrew O'Rouke ran along the edge of the High Street, in the rain, when he lost his footing on the slippery kerb and fell under the wheels of a double-decker bus. An inquisitive crowd soon gathered, although no-one really wanted to see what had become of him.

There was great sympathy for the apologetic, shaking, bus driver. He knew it wasn't his fault, just the wet pavement and the man hurrying. The police arrived, then the ambulance. One of the paramedics looked down and said "Poor Bugger." No-one argued with him.

James Andrew O'Rouke arrived at the hospital, there was no point in rushing him into casualty. The staff looked through his wallet for his details. The police knocked and rang as they stood on his wet doorstep. The knocking echoed and the phone rang in the home of James Andrew O'Rouke, but there was no reply.

Inside, resting against a vase of Chrysanthemums was a letter for James Andrew O'Rouke from his wife. He would never read it, would never know that on that very day, she had packed a bag and phoned for a taxi. He would never know that at the moment his heart stopped, she was boarding a flight to go to the man she'd been having an affair with.

At the hospital, the staff looked for more clues to his identity. In his wallet was an appointment card for one of their own departments. Consultant Norman Jones was due to see James Andrew O'Rouke that very afternoon. That was why he had been hurrying along the road, he'd hoped to catch the very bus that killed him.

At 1.30, a nurse called for James Andrew O'Rouke three times before telling the doctor that he had not arrived. Norman Jones was both annoyed and relieved. It meant that another appointment would be needed, but also that the bad news could wait. James Andrew O'Rouke had not looked like a sick man, but the cancer growing in his brain was accelerating. It would be a shock to James Andrew O'Rouke, who had no idea, he'd just wondering why he was becoming unsteady on his feet.

The staff found the business card of James Andrew O'Rouke and phoned his company, but the phone rang unanswered. Paul Johnson, company director, was not answering. He'd locked his office door after the call from the bank and was working through a bottle of whisky. At 4.30 he'd have to meet the staff. The promised orders had not materialised and the company was gone. There would be no wages, no pensions and no redundancy money.

James Andrew O'Rouke lay on his slab, cleaned up as best they could. His clothes and belongings were locked away waiting collection. They put a cover over James Andrew O'Rouke to wheel him to the cold store. One of them looked at the face of James Andrew O'Rouke and thought he had the hint of a smile. "Poor bugger." he said. "He never knew what was about to hit him."

A Modern Fairy Tale

A poor but kindly man walked through the town. He'd spent all his cash in Iceland and was walking home to await the shopping's delivery van.

It was early November and the rain was pouring down. A cold north wind made him wrap his thin denim jacket tighter round his scrawny body.

As he held his head down to keep the rain out of his eyes he saw a two pound coin on the pavement, shining like gold through the grime. He looked around but everyone was rushing past so he quickly reached down and grabbed it. He dried it on his hands and dropped it into his pocket where it clanged quietly against his keys. He thought about what to do with it, maybe chocolate for his golden haired daughter, football stickers for his golden haired son, a juicy bone for his golden retriever or a scented shampoo for his greasy haired wife. He even considered buying something for himself, but couldn't think of anything he wanted for £2.

As he approached the clock tower, three people were eagerly awaiting his arrival. A child with rain, or something, dripping from his nose was standing beside an old buggy. Inside was strangely stuffed filthy yellow baby-grow topped by a dented football wearing a hideous Halloween mask. A handwritten sign, with spelling mistakes said 'Pennie four the gy.' The rain had caused streaks of cleanliness down his cheeks and he added 'Please Mister' to the message.

Next to the boy was a youth sitting on the pavement. His head was down as he huddled in his old anorak. His sign was at least better spelt 'Homeless – dog to feed.' Sure enough at his side was the wettest, ugliest dog the man had ever seen. It's eyes staring at its owner's baseball cap in front of them that contained a few copper coins.

Next to the child, and the youth and his dog, stood an old lady. Tiny but standing upright, she wore a black raincoat and plastic hood. In front of her she carried a tray of Remembrance Day poppies that was beginning to fill with water. She looked at him through thick misted glasses..

'Oh hell' thought the man, wishing he hadn't picked up the coin. He had no other cash on him and could have smiled apologetically and walked on. But the £2 coin was suddenly very heavy in his pocket. He just knew that they all knew he had money and that they all deserved it. He tried to look away and his eyes fixed on a sign outside a shop. They sold lottery tickets.

He would buy a scratch-card and it if won he would divide the prize by four and everyone would profit. A huge weight was lifted from him as he rushed into the shop and purchased the ticket. Inside he rubbed the card with his door key to see what he had won…

Don't be ridiculous. This is a fairy story not a miracle.

Ruth Partis

The Fossil Man

He returned to the blank page on his computer. He'd done everything he could to delay actually doing what he had to do. He'd read his E-mails, he's checked his Facebook. He's even collected up all the paper re-cycling and put it outside in the bin. He'd had two cups of coffee and eaten a banana. But, it really was now time to write the report for the local paper on last night's meeting.

It was quite a simple task really; at least it would have been if he'd actually been at the meeting. He'd been there at the start – he'd collected the entrance money, but once the lights went down and the speaker started his talk with slides, he's whispered to his neighbour that he had a message from home and had to leave. He'd got to his armchair just in time to see the start of the football match he'd wanted to watch.

In the darkness no-one would have seen him go and he'd quite happily missed the talk about 'Fossil Hunting in Kent.' His father had been a fossil hunter too and he'd got enough horrific memories of rain and windswept beaches and shoe boxes filled with labelled bits of fossil, to last a lifetime.

He wrote 'Members viewed the slides with great interest and were excited to actually touch the real pieces of fossil that the speaker passed round. They were amazed to hear that they had been found under cliffs very near their homes. The speaker was entertaining and very knowledgeable about his subject. He was warmly applauded and thanked for his talk by members.'

He thought that was grovelling enough about what was probably a very tedious talk. He continued ' Afterwards members enjoyed tea and biscuits and the meeting closed at 9.30pm. The speaker at the next meeting will be....'

He stopped writing at this. He hadn't a clue who the next speaker was. He checked his Facebook page again, and his E-mails but he couldn't face another cup of coffee.

He checked the messages on his phone then dialled a friend who was at the meeting and casually asked him who the speaker was to be at the next meeting.

"It's the Fossil Man." He replied.

"What again?" He spluttered.

"Well yes, after the hall's power failure, we asked him to come back next month. Where were you? I looked for you as we went out but someone said you'd gone home. We all went to the pub to watch the match. We had a great evening. Terrific atmosphere."

Ashes to Sunshine

Marie watched the car go round the corner and went back to her husband, Paul. He was sitting silently with his head in his hands. Their visitors, his uncle and aunt had just told them that his mother was dead and cremated, her ashes scattered on a garden there.

He had been brought up by his grandmother and had always had a difficult relationship with her. "They should have told me before," he said bitterly.

She agreed, but had an idea to try to make him feel better.

The next day they drove the forty odd miles to the crematorium; they hadn't been to that one before. When they got out the car they were stunned by the beautiful gardens. Flowers were everywhere in the sunshine and there was a huge pond with exotic carp just under the surface. They sat on a bench and watched them for ages. Birds were singing in the trees and butterflies and bees were feeding all over a lavender hedge behind them. The bees buzzing totally blocked out the sound of the nearby main road.

After a while they continued round the winding path beside a huge rose garden. They came to a glass chapel where visitors could place cut flowers and they added the bunch they had bought on the way,

A large crowd of not too upset mourners was gathered at the entrance to a closed chapel, A hearse arrived covered in wreathes and bouquets, the biggest spelt out' Nan' and 'Mum.' The big doors were opened and the family went inside. Marie and Paul looked at each other and without a word slipped into the back and stood with the others who couldn't get a seat.

The service was simple but lovely, the tune 'Lara's Theme' was played. The hymn 'Morning has broken' was sung, a delightful poem written by a small grandchild was read and simple prayers prayed. In just a short while, the song 'Raining in my Heart' was played and Marie and Paul found themselves outside shaking a priest's hand and congratulating him on the service. They managed to slip past the family and hid round the corner giggling like teenagers. They didn't feel at all guilty, and no-one seemed to have noticed them.

They had another walk round the grounds. Marie was so pleased to see that Paul was obviously feeling better. It was a beautiful place and it would be hard to feel depressed there.

Paul explained that he had often had to visit his mother as he had grown up, in various awful places, filthy squats, stark clinics, stark hospitals wards and twice in terrifying prisons. Every time there had been promises of better things to come, promises that were never kept. "I can finally go away leaving her somewhere really beautiful," he said "And move on." And so they did, starting with steak and chips at a nearby pub.

Ruth Partis

Family Secrets

After she died, in with my mother's paperwork I found a big envelope made of strong brown paper. There was nothing written on it and I so wish that I hadn't opened it, but I had to really, in case it was something important.

On the top was a document I recognised. My own birth certificate, but that gave me no surprises. I knew that I had been born before my parents married and that on the certificate no father was named. I had known this since the first time I had needed to show my birth certificate and it had never bothered me. I expect it was a social disaster when I was born, but now no-one turns a hair.

I tipped out the rest of the contents on to the table in front of me. It was a whole load of papers that I had never seen before. There was a photograph of my mother with a man I recognised. Not the man I had called Dad for my whole life but a man known to me, and to almost everyone in this country.

There were also dozens of newspaper cutting about the man and all the things he had done. One headline described him as the most evil man in the country, and as I read the cuttings I could see why.

There were also letters from him to my mother that left my parentage in no doubt. The information hit me suddenly. This man, hated by everyone, was my father.

No wonder my mother had never told me. I wondered why she had kept the photo and the cutting, I wish she hadn't.

I sat for a long time wondering what to do, I imagined my mother doing the same many years before. Finally I took the coward's way out. I did exactly what she had done. I carefully put all the cuttings, the letters and the photograph back in the envelope and put them with my own certificates and papers. On the outside of the envelope I wrote just one word 'Sorry.' And I left it for my children to find after I died

Also Published By TAUP

James Apps   And Darkly Glows The City
Stories From The Darkside
The Kowhai and Me
The Professor and his Son - Zradian Chronicles
The Reluctant Hero - Zradian Chronicles
The-Doomsday-Bomb - Zradian Chronicles

Peter Apps   Across The Continuum Sea
Deja Vu To The Nth
Disastrous Science
Earth Against Earth
Fracture Point
Meanwhile In Time
Time Askew
The Growing Universe

Malcolm Gibbs   The Island Gang Narratives

Gordon Henderson   A Walk to the Duck Pond and Other Poems
Litter Angels
Operation Seal Island
Pigeon Pie And Other Tasty Tales

Ruth Partis   Numbers

Jeremy Thornton   Praise And Applause

Sheppey Writers   Quirky Humans And Others